The Chianti
Chronicles

Volume One:
Fictional Tales of Vietnam Vets

Publishing Services provided by Paper Raven Books LLC

Printed in the United States of America

First Printing, 2023

Paperback ISBN: 979-8-9881562-1-5
Hardback ISBN: 979-8-9881562-0-8

For my beautiful wife, Miss Kim

Contents

Introduction

'm Mary Beth Czubay, author of *Easy Out on Third: Raising a Child With Special Needs*. I wrote that book because I had a meaningful story to tell, and I hoped my experience would help other parents who are dealing with this very challenging situation. I was humbled when my older brother Kevin Cullen asked me to provide an introduction to his first book. Kevin has always had a gift for and an interest in writing, and he is an exceptional story teller. He recently retired after serving twenty-seven years in the U. S. Air Force, followed by many years in the corporate world. That enabled him to finally turn a lifelong dream and hobby into a realty with his series of fictional short stories, *The Chianti Chronicles*.

In this first Volume—*Fictional Tales of Vietnam Vets*—Kevin tells ten captivating stories of brave veterans who take on life after serving in Vietnam. He drew from his wide range of military and personal experiences, along with observations from his life journey. These stories will capture your interest from the very beginning. Each one is truly unique and so believable with surprising twists and turns along the way. You will feel like you know the characters personally as relatives or friends. You will also experience their wide range of emotions from pain to joy. Not to sound too cliché, but "I laughed, I cried…" You know the drill.

Please pour yourself a nice beverage such as a cup of hot tea, a cold beer, or (of course) a glass of Chianti. Then get comfortable and lose yourself in these wonderful stories and take a break from your own reality.

Kevin, thank you for including me in the early part of your journey as an author, and thanks for creating these fascinating tales. I can't wait for the next volume!

—*Mary Beth Czubay*

Ominous Anticipation

THE SPIRITUALITY OF PLAYING CATCH

A fatigued Grampa Jake poured a fresh glass of Chianti, then slowly sank into his massive recliner, which he affectionately referred to as Beatrice. It was a warm and sunny Saturday afternoon in August 1969. Jake lived in base housing at Fort Dix, New Jersey with his daughter-in-law and grandson, while his son, Joseph, was serving in Vietnam. He had just finished an extensive "honey-do" list for his daughter-in-law, and he was ready to relax and watch the Mets game.

Jake took a long, slow sip of his Chianti, then briefly closed his eyes as he oozed into a well-deserved nap. As he zoned out, he felt a presence nearby. He opened his eyes to see his nine-year-old grandson, Kirk, standing next to his chair. He wore the Mets baseball cap Jake had bought for him last Christmas and held two baseball gloves and a ball.

"Hey, buddy, what's up?"

Kirk smiled. "Do you want to play catch with me, Grampa?"

Pretending to frown, Jake teased, "With *you*?"

Kirk laughed, the beautiful sound warming Jake's heart. "Ha ha. Come on, Grampa, let's go."

Jake reached over and tousled Kirk's hair. "Do you know that you're a cool dude with an attitude?"

"You always ask me that, Grampa." He then tossed the bigger glove in Jake's lap and hurried out back, yelling, "Come on, hurry up."

Jake shifted mental gears, laboriously parted ways with Beatrice, then turned the game off. He headed out to the backyard with Kirk, and they immersed themselves into one of the most satisfying spiritual rituals known to mankind—playing catch. To an outsider looking in, it probably appeared to be boring. But, for those involved, it was like being part of a synergistic symphony. Accurately throwing the ball back and forth to each other, with that unique sound of the glove popping when the ball was properly caught right in the pocket, was special. You could also mix it up.

"Grampa, throw me some 'Texas Leaguers' so that I can make diving catches."

"I'm worried you'll get grass stains on your clothes, buddy. Then we'll have to face the wrath of your mom."

"It's okay, Grampa. You've seen me doing my own laundry. I'll take care of it."

He reached down to scoop up a low throw from Kirk. "Okay, I remember."

Rhythmically, they threw the ball back and forth.

"Nice scoop, Grampa. You remember what Dad told me before he left for Vietnam, right? He told me to step up and

2

help Mom out. I need to make my bed every morning, take out the trash, help Mom wash dishes, and stuff like that."

Grampa Kirk acknowledged that wisdom. "And that was sound advice. Okay, then, let's do some Texas Leaguers."

Laser-focused in the defensive fielding position with his gloved hand on his left knee and his bare hand on the right, Kirk shouted, "Hey, batter batter!"

Jake then tossed a variety of fairly difficult-to-catch high balls, and Kirk was up for the challenge. His grampa's throws were coming back at him quickly. A good healthy sweat going, Kirk raced back and forth and side to side. He caught a few and missed a few diving attempts, getting grass stains on his t-shirt and shorts. It was a beautiful sight to see a vibrant and hopeful young boy, enjoying what would certainly be a profound memory later in life.

After about thirty minutes, a panting Kirk yelled, "Hey, Grampa, let's go get a lemonade."

"That's a great idea, buddy. Let's do it."

They headed inside to grab their drinks, then sat out back on the family picnic table on the deck.

REFLECTING OVER LEMONADE

"Grampa, was my dad a good baseball player?"

"He sure was. He had talent, but he worked hard at hitting, catching, and throwing."

"Am I a good ball player, Grampa?"

As Kirk patiently awaited this critical evaluation, Grampa Jake paused with purpose, put on a stern-looking face, crossed his arms, then grimaced slightly. "Well, Kirk, you're at least as good as your dad was at nine, maybe a little bit better. And the sky's the limit if you work hard at it like your dad did."

Kirk's facial expression shifted from concern to absolute happiness with a wide smile. They sat silently for a few minutes. Then Kirk said, "I can't wait until Dad gets home from Vietnam. I miss him a lot."

"Me too, buddy, on both counts."

"Why is he fighting in that war anyway?"

"Well, he's a career soldier, and he's fighting for our country, and us. The military is stopping the spread of Communism."

Nervously, Kirk tapped the table as he slowly took another sip of his lemonade. pondering what Grampa just told him.

Kirk's mom yelled out the back door, "Come on in and wash up, guys. Dinner's ready. I made meatloaf, mashed potatoes, and green beans."

Upon heading into the kitchen, Kirk and Jake faced a stern greeting from Mom. "Kirk, you got grass stains all over your clothes. I hope we can wash them out. Go ahead and change and bring them back to me so I can soak them."

"I'm sorry, Mom. Grampa was throwing me Texas Leaguers, and I had to dive to catch them."

Mom asked, "What's a Texas Leaguer, buddy?"

"It's a high blooper that can fall between an outfielder and an infielder for a hit if I don't catch it. I made a bunch of great catches on them today, didn't I, Grampa?"

"You sure did, Kirk. You have a great glove."

Mom smiled. "You're an awesome baseball player, buddy. Now go ahead and change your clothes and wash up for dinner."

MILITARY DEATH NOTIFICATIONS

After taking a quick peek at the meatloaf in the oven, Mom said, "Thanks, Jake, for playing catch with Kirk. He's missing Joseph so much, and it's nice to have a male presence in the house."

Grampa Jake walked over to his daughter-in-law and placed a comforting hand on her shoulder. "Are you okay, Tina? I know you're feeling a high level of stress while Joseph is in Nam, but you've seemed different the past few days."

Lip trembling, Tina took a deep breath. "There's a neighbor down the street who I really don't know. I was driving home from the commissary the other day, and as I passed her house, a military vehicle pulled up. Two soldiers in full uniform got out and walked up to her front door. I found out later she received a formal death notification. Her husband was killed in action. I don't think I could handle that, Jake."

Tina sobbed, and Jake stood silently as he hugged his shaken daughter-in-law. Every family awaiting the return of their soldier fighting overseas feared the thought of a military vehicle pulling into their driveway, followed by two soldiers walking up to their door. The military went to great lengths to ensure they were done with the utmost dignity and respect, but they *were* death notifications.

Interrupting that silent moment, Kirk entered the room and yelled, "How's your potassium level, Grampa?"

Grampa Jake shrugged his shoulders and smirked. "It's actually kind of low, buddy. Looks like I may need to have some ice cream after dinner."

Whenever he saw an opportunity to eat ice cream with his grandson, Grampa Jake claimed his potassium level was low.

"Hey, Mom, can me and Grampa have ice cream after dinner?"

"You sure can, buddy, but you have to eat your green beans, okay?"

Kirk nodded with a big smile on his face.

ICE CREAM AND A BOY'S CURIOSITY

Since Kirk's dad left for Vietnam about nine months ago, his mom and his grampa did their best to shield Kirk from the ominous sense of fear they were experiencing. After a great dinner at which Kirk ate his green beans, Mom prepared two identical double scoops in sugar cones—one scoop of vanilla and one scoop of chocolate. They sat together on the picnic table, thoroughly enjoying their guilty pleasure.

Kirk told Grampa Jake, "I'm glad you, me, and Dad are all Mets fans. Do you think they can win the World Series?"

"It's going to be tough, Kirk, but you never know. Maybe a miracle will happen."

"So, you were a soldier too, Grampa?"

"Yes. I was in World War II."

"Was it scary?"

"It sure was, but we were trained and confident. We felt like we had the best military in the world."

"Were you trying to stop the Communists like Dad is doing?"

"No, buddy, we were fighting the Nazis, and we beat them soundly just like your Little League team did against the Giants last week."

"Did you have to kill anyone while you were in the war?"

Grampa looked up, then carefully responded, "Let me just say that we all did what we had to do to win and get home safely."

Although he was only nine, Kirk could sense he touched on a difficult subject. "That's good, Grampa. I'm glad you did."

They both nodded as they finished up their delicious ice creams in silence.

THE POWER OF WORDS

Kirk broke the silence. "Thanks for playing catch with me. It was fun."

"Anything for you, Kirk."

"Anything? Okay, give me a million dollars."

"If I had a million dollars, they'd be all yours, buddy."

They both laughed. Then Kirk asked, "Can we go inside and do the Word Jumbles from today's paper?"

"Sounds like a great idea."

Once indoors, Grampa Jake refilled his wine glass with a fresh pour of Chianti, grabbed that day's newspaper, and returned to the comfort of Beatrice. Kirk joined him in the chair with a fresh lemonade in hand. They then began their challenging but fun mental workout, a ritual since Jake moved in with Kirk and his mom. Although just a young child, Kirk developed an impressive proficiency at finding words from the jumbled letters. The first combination was: C U R I C S. Kirk and Grampa Jake fumbled for a few minutes; then Kirk shouted, "CIRCUS!"

"Boom, you got it, buddy!"

The next combination was: Y A K K A, and after a brief think, Jake said, "I got it! KAYAK."

Kirk clapped his hands, pumped his fist in the air, and shouted, "Yes!"

They then finished the final two scrambles and relaxed for a few minutes.

Kirk told his Grampa, "I love words. It's so much fun figuring out the Word Jumbles."

"Yes, it is fun, and I think we're getting pretty good at it."

"Yes, we are, Grampa."

Grampa Jake reiterated an important life lesson for Kirk. "Just remember words are powerful—both positively and negatively. What you say and how you say it are important. And once you say something, it's hard to take it back. The old adage 'Silence is golden' is a smart way to go. The best way I can put it is to treat people with dignity and respect."

After a silent pause, Kirk asked, "Do you miss Gramma?"

"I sure do. She was my wife for thirty-one years when she got sick. She was also my best friend. I think about her every day."

"Do you think she's in heaven, Grampa?"

"I know she is, buddy. She's probably playing BINGO with a bunch of angels."

At that point, the doorbell rang, and Kirk's mom yelled, "Kirk, Robbie and Nick are here. They want to play baseball with you for a little while before it gets dark."

Kirk hugged his Grampa, then yelled, "I'm coming, Mom!"

Kirk grabbed his bag with his baseball stuff: several balls, his bat, and his glove. He put on his Mets hat, then hopped on his bike and headed out to the park down the street with his buddies. Focused on getting to their destination and playing as much baseball as possible, the boys were oblivious to the ominous military vehicle headed to Kirk's house.

A SOLDIER RETURNS HOME

Kirk and his buddies played for about an hour when it started to get dark. They had a great time, and they were feeling good as they headed back to their homes on their bikes. That same military vehicle passed them again, but in the opposite direction.

Kirk's house was the closest to the park. As he approached, his friends shouted their goodbyes. Kirk pulled into his drive-way, then put his bike and baseball equipment in the garage. He entered the house and saw Mom and Grampa sitting in the living room. Mom was crying, and Grampa was nervously clenching and unclenching his fists.

"What's going on?'

His mom and Grampa Jake looked up at him but did not respond.

Kirk yelled, "What happened?"

At that point, a voice from the hallway quietly said, "Hey, buddy. I missed you. Come on over here and give me a hug."

It was his father, dressed in his formal military uniform, wearing a patch over his left eye and leaning on a crutch.

Kirk ran to him, shouting, "Dad! Are you okay? What happened?"

As his son hugged him tightly, Kirk's dad cried tears of joy. "Your mom chastised me for not calling ahead, but I wanted to surprise you. I'm home for good, Kirk. I was injured in battle, and they sent me home early, and it's so great to be home. I love you."

THE END

Slow Dancing at the Clamdiggers Saloon

THE DAY AFTER AND THE DAY OF

On a tranquil Long Island morning, Derek Williamson sat on his family's dock sipping coffee, taking in the comforting smell of the salt air, and enjoying the serene view of Great South Bay. A hard thud from behind him on the nearby deck interrupted him.

"Ouch!"

Derek turned around. His fully dressed father was lying under their picnic table in the fetal position, surrounded by crushed beer cans. Derek quickly headed toward him.

"What the hell, Pop?"

Getting up, his disheveled father rubbed his head, and sat at the table. "Could you fix me a coffee, son?"

It was five a.m. on Friday, October 17, 1969, the day after the New York Mets won their first World Series. The day of Derek's enlistment in the U.S. Army.

Derek went inside the house and got his father's coffee. "Here you go, Pop."

His father asked, "What time should we leave for Fort Dix?"

"Around two. We need to get there by five. I'm making breakfast bowls, and don't forget lunch at Uncle Joey's later."

Derek's best friend, Freddie, arrived, poured himself a coffee, and joined Derek and his father at the picnic table. They discussed the prior day, specifically the Mets' win and Derek's sendoff.

After a while, Derek excused himself, went to his bedroom, and sat on his bed. He admired the beautiful young lady lying there, Regina O'Leary. The eighteen-year-old Derek loved her, though they seemed ill-fated. They had dated for two years but broke up over a year ago after the first of two calamities. Recently, they had secretly resumed dating.

Derek gently kissed her. "You told me to wake you before six." A groggy Regina nodded. "I made coffee, and I'm cooking breakfast bowls. I'll be in the kitchen."

As Derek cooked, Regina walked in and wrapped her arms around him from behind.

"Stay for breakfast, Regina."

"That's tempting, but I can't. It's too risky; my parents would freak. I want to see Freddie, so I'll have a quick coffee." She kissed his neck. "Last night was nice."

The previous evening, Regina attended Derek's farewell at the Clamdiggers Saloon and after a few drinks, she slow danced with Derek, setting off sparks. They exited at an opportune moment for a fervent exchange before sleeping.

"I love you, Regina." She hugged Derek tighter, and he closed his eyes. "I'm going to miss you, but your parents hate me. Plus, I'll likely go to Nam. Please don't wait for me; move on."

Regina lightly punched Derek's back. "I did not hear that, Derek Williamson. I'm going to miss so much about you, but I'll miss slow dancing at the Saloon the most. I feel so secure when we slow dance."

With a deep sigh, Derek replied, "You drive me crazy."

They went outside and enjoyed a relaxing conversation over coffee.

Freddie toasted, "To my three favorite people in the world!"

None of them would see Derek again for some time.

CLAM DIGGING

In the prior summer of '68, Derek and Freddie bought a dilapidated clam boat, which they named *Titanic II.* Tired of dead-end jobs, they fixed it up and made money clam digging, manually harvesting clams from below the surface of the flats. The *Titanic II* was a flatbed clam boat, and they used long clam-tongs, like massive scissors with interlocking teeth-hinged rakes at the bottom. After digging all day, they sorted, bagged, and tagged their harvest for sale at a commercial dock.

DEREK AND REGINA

Derek was ruggedly handsome with long blond hair. An only child, he lived with his father, Charlie Williamson. At fourteen, Derek's beloved mother, Emily, was shot during a convenience store robbery. After her death, Derek's father eventually inherited an adequate financial sum, which helped them survive, but he resorted to heavy drinking. When Derek entered high school in September 1965, his situation—a murdered mother and a drunkard father—embarrassed him, but he endured.

Regina O'Leary was an Irish beauty with dark brown hair and piercing green eyes. Despite her petite frame, she had a strong emotional psyche. Her exceptional intellectual and social abilities enabled her to excel in high school. Unlike Derek, she was born into affluent privilege.

As a sophomore, Derek was an honors student and starting linebacker on the varsity football team, on track for several academic awards and scholarships. He was balancing his dysfunctional world when he met Regina, who was writing an article in the school paper about Derek making varsity as a sophomore. Their friendship evolved into a frenzied period of sexual discovery. But Regina's wealthy parents looked down on Derek, as he didn't meet their standards. Though Derek tried to please them, after two difficult years, things blew up.

CALAMITY #1 - THE PROM DEBACLE

On the evening of Regina's and Derek's junior prom, the O'Learys hosted a photo session/cocktail party, and reluctantly invited Derek's father. Unfortunately, he showed up intoxicated, spilled a drink, and tipped a tray of Swedish meatballs on their carpet.

Regina's father couldn't contain his scorn. "Damn white trash."

Derek pointed his finger at Regina's father. "Hey, fuck you, man! It was an accident." He and his father stormed out.

After that traumatic experience, Derek broke up with Regina and quit school.

CALAMITY #2 - CHRISTOPHER GETS A BEATING

Begrudgingly, a heartbroken Regina accepted Derek's decision, eventually caving to her parents and dating their preference, Christopher Sawyer. Meanwhile, Derek focused on making money clamming and cooking. That summer and the '68-'69 school year flew by, and the Lindenhurst High seniors were excited about graduating. Earning money and doing what he loved, Derek felt no remorse as a high school dropout.

In the summer of '69, an acquaintance convinced Freddie and Derek to attend a pool party. Unbeknownst to them, it was at Christopher Sawyer's house. When they arrived, they saw Regina and Christopher and tried to leave quietly. A drunken Christopher saw Derek and razzed him about being a dropout with a drunkard father. Some in attendance laughed, while others were shocked, considering Derek's legendary status as a high school athlete. Regina told Christopher to stop.

After a moment of mental paralysis, Derek stormed over and shoved Christopher, who pushed back and said, "Get the hell out of here, lowlife."

Derek shouted, "Lowlife *this*, bitch!" and beat Christopher with a flurry of punches. Derek was strong from digging clams, so several guys had to pull him off a bloodied Christopher. Derek was taken away in cuffs, Christopher in an ambulance.

Derek was charged with assault and went to court in mid-August. After mixed inputs from witnesses, they negotiated a deal. The families would split Christopher's medical bills, and Derek would join the military instead of jail time. Regina broke up with Christopher.

THE CLAMDIGGERS SALOON

Derek's Uncle Joey was his mother's older brother and a World War II veteran. As a returning soldier, he earned low-interest loans and one year of unemployment compensation. He capitalized and built a massive three-story structure.

Joey had a clear vision: a spacious residence on the top floor, a nightclub on the second floor, and a seafood restaurant with an elaborate kitchen on the first floor. He even installed an elevator. Since his property straddled a corner of the bay and a canal, he also built an L-shaped dock where customers could dock their boats to dine and party.

Joey and his wife never had kids, so Derek was like their son, especially after his mother's death. Derek had great memories from the Saloon, including the nights he and Regina stopped by to dance. Great local musicians played on weekends, and "Unchained Melody" was their favorite song.

On Derek's final morning at home before enlisting, he arrived at the Saloon for some alone time with Uncle Joey. It was comfortable outside, so they had coffee on the dock. They talked about the previous day, specifically the Miracle Mets winning the World Series and Derek's sendoff at the Saloon with family and friends.

Derek grabbed his uncle's shoulder. "Thanks for the tremendous party last night."

"My pleasure, Derek. I gotta be honest—I miss watching you play football. You were special. And I feel terrible about you and Regina. If it wasn't for all this crap, you might be playing for Syracuse on a scholarship this year. Now you might go to Nam."

"My thing with Regina is complicated. She's got a beautiful spell on me I can't shake."

Wearing a stern expression, Uncle Joey leaned forward. "Let me be straight. Do you love Regina?" Overwhelmed, Derek looked down and cried, and Uncle Joey hugged him. "We adore her and wish you didn't have to deal with her family's nonsense. One big thing. If you're interested, we want you to have this place when we retire. We built a solid nest egg, and we're moving to Florida in a few years. You're a talented chef, and you can live a nice life here. Get through this situation and see how you feel when you return, okay?"

"Yes, sir, Uncle Joey. Wow, I don't know what to say. I'm not sure I deserve that."

"Derek, you don't need to say a thing, and you absolutely deserve it. I'm proud of you for a lot of reasons. And one reason is how you're taking your medicine like a man. Please be careful if you wind up in Vietnam. It's insane over there. Don't be a hero."

VIETNAM

Derek completed basic training at Fort Dix, was assigned to the 101st Airborne Division, and went to Vietnam in the spring of 1970 for a one-year tour of duty. As a combat infantryman, Derek survived with a "kill or be killed" instinct.

His toughest combat experience was A Shau Valley, a strategic focal point for the North Vietnamese Army (NVA). In 1970, the 101st Airborne Division was tasked with regaining control of the valley. NVA troops attacked the outnumbered American troops using a barrage of attacks, and seventy-five U.S. soldiers were killed.

In an interview with the military newspaper, *Stars and Stripes*, Derek said, "Being under constant fire was intense. Several B-52 bombers dropped napalm in our area. You can smell it, and you can taste it."

Derek earned the Bronze Star for "displaying heroic actions while encountering enemy hostile fire. His actions saved at least twelve lives." During his time there, Regina sent twelve letters (one each month) to Derek in Nam, but he didn't respond to any of them.

A REUNION WITH REGINA

After Vietnam, Sergeant Williamson was assigned to Fort Jackson in South Carolina and took leave enroute in Lindenhurst. Derek's father, Uncle Joey, and Freddie informed the mayor that a Bronze Star recipient—and a Lindenhurst native—would be in town, so city officials organized a ceremony at the Lindy Docks. Regina, now a sophomore at Hofstra University, decided to go.

Derek was excited about taking some R&R and possibly seeing Regina. He also wanted to go clamming on the *Titanic II* with Freddie and cook and party at the Saloon.

The ceremony kicked off with the Lindy High band performing. Then the mayor, Derek's father, Uncle Joey, and Freddie each spoke of the town's pride in Derek. Derek's high school football coach, a Korean War veteran, mentioned Derek's exceptional athleticism and his courageous military service. He asked Derek, who was wearing his formal military uniform, to join him onstage.

The coach concluded, "Derek, I'm proud of your courage in earning the prestigious Bronze Star."

They exchanged military salutes and hugged.

As Derek took his turn to speak, he spotted Regina in the audience. Regina was smiling, and Derek hoped she was impressed by his accomplishments. Derek spoke passionately about his love for his hometown and his fond memories growing up on the bay. He thanked his father, his uncle, and Freddie for their support. He mentioned his fellow warriors, especially those who didn't survive the harrowing violence of Vietnam. In tears, he concluded by talking about his beautiful mother. "I feel deprived that she wasn't with me during some important times, including today. Don't worry, Mom. I'll make you proud by living a good life."

Derek's Uncle Joey wrapped up by inviting everyone to the Clamdiggers Saloon for happy hour with complimentary hors d'oeuvres. He also coyly mentioned the discounted Friday Night Seafood Special and how the popular DJ, Lenny B the Long Island Lunatic, would be spinning tunes.

As the ceremony ended, Derek greeted Regina with a hug. They chatted briefly, and Derek invited her to meet him at the Saloon. First, he went home to change into comfortable clothes.

After happy hour, Freddie and Derek's father joined Regina and Derek at an inside table for dinner. His aunt and uncle stopped by for a quick drink and some light conversation, then left to take care of their customers. Everyone relished the pleasant experience.

Freddie said, "Wow. The four of us haven't been together since the morning Derek left for basic training." He held up his glass. "Another toast to my favorite people in the world, you three."

Derek's dad and Freddie headed upstairs to check out the DJ, and Derek and Regina moved to the outside dock.

Derek ordered a bottle of Chianti, and a wide-eyed Regina said with a smirk, "Wow, look at you, Mister Wine Connoisseur."

"I was in Nam with an Italian kid from Brooklyn, Louie Fierro. He introduced me to wine on an R&R trip to Thailand. He really knew his shit, and he especially loved a nice Chianti. Great guy."

"Well, I'd love to meet him," Regina replied.

Derek looked somberly over the bay. "Unfortunately, he didn't make it."

They sat in silence until their waiter returned with their wine, and Regina took her first ever sip of Chianti.

"I really like it." She held up her glass. "Here's a toast to you, Sergeant Williamson, my favorite soldier and my hero."

Clinking glasses, they took a sip.

Regina then asked, "So how are you, Derek?"

"I'm well. It's nice to spend time with you. I wasn't sure if we'd see each other again. How about you, Regina? How are you?"

"I'm doing great, now that I'm with you. Today was impressive."

Derek thanked her, then tenderly tucked a strand of her hair behind her ear. "My God, you look more beautiful than ever. Freddie told me you were dating some 'Frat Boy.'"

Laughing softly at his apparent jealousy, Regina waved her hand. "He doesn't mean anything to me. My parents are matchmaking again."

"Damn, I missed you."

"Why didn't you respond to my letters, Derek? That broke my heart."

Derek got emotional, then looked away for a moment to regain his composure. "I never opened them because I didn't think I would survive, but I still have them. By the way, I love that you wrote 'Slow Dancing at the Clamdiggers Saloon' on each envelope. Someday, I'll read them, Regina—I promise. I just couldn't do it over there. I tried not to think about you, but I did."

Derek grabbed Regina's hand and kissed it as they admired the glimmering view of the sun setting over the bay. Momentarily, the two soulmates were at peace.

The DJ on the second floor announced the next song, "Unchained Melody," via the Saloon's speakers.

A slightly tipsy Regina stood up. "May I have this dance, Sergeant Williamson?"

Standing, Derek pulled Regina close to him. She felt Derek's physical strength, and he felt Regina's inner strength. They savored being physically and emotionally close, even for a moment. As they slow danced, Derek kissed her neck, took in her fragrance, and stroked his hand up and down her lower back. When the song ended, a flustered Derek told Regina he was heading to his empty home and he would love it if she joined him. She agreed without hesitation, and they escaped for a few intimate hours together.

THE MORNING AFTER, AGAIN

In the middle of the night, Regina tried to quietly sneak out, but Derek woke up. "Hey, you."

"I need to go. You know the situation."

Derek sat up. "Regina, I'm taking control. We need to be together. I came close to dying several times over there, and I'm a bit fucked up mentally, but I'm not crazy. I refuse to lose you again. I need to go to South Carolina on Monday for a year to complete my military commitment, but I promise to keep in touch, and I want to be with you when I return. Your parents need to accept that. I plan to work with Uncle Joey and learn more about the restaurant business after my discharge. We can do this. We're in love, right?"

A tearful Regina, looking as if the weight of the world had lifted off her shoulders, responded, "Yes, Derek, we're in love. We're so in love."

The following morning, Derek decided to do something daring. He called Regina's father and asked to meet. Mr. O'Leary agreed and asked that Derek's father and his Uncle Joey join them. They met over lunch at the Saloon.

After tense greetings, Regina's father stood, addressing Derek's father. "Sir, what I said the evening of Regina's and Derek's prom was disrespectful. I apologize from the bottom of my heart. Please forgive me."

Derek's father shook hands without saying a word.

Regina's father faced Derek. "On that unfortunate evening, I admired you because of how you defended your father's honor." He then proposed a toast. "To Sergeant Derek Williamson, for your courageous service. Congratulations. We're very proud of you."

The tension subsided, and Derek stood up, clearing his throat. "Well, sir, I'm glad you said that. I wanted to talk with you because I plan to ask your daughter to marry me, and I'm respectfully requesting your permission. I love Regina, and I can't live without her."

Regina's father gave Derek his blessing during a great seafood lunch. Derek later bought a ring and drove to Regina's home that evening in his dress uniform.

He knelt on one knee in front of her family. "Regina, would you please be my bride?"

Regina said yes.

SEPARATION, MARRIAGE, AND SATURDAY NIGHTS

Regina and Derek enjoyed the rest of that weekend, including catching a Mets game on Sunday. Upon discussing their plans, they decided to have a small wedding on Monday, October 16, 1972—the third anniversary of the Mets' miraculous World Series win.

In the meantime, Derek headed down to Fort Jackson in South Carolina to complete his remaining one-year military obligation as a drill sergeant. He earned the respect of everyone up and down his chain of command. His combat experience was revered, and his firm but fair approach with recruits helped reinforce his credibility. A few times, he traveled to New York on leave to see his loved ones, but his final trip was to attend his father's funeral when he died of a heart attack.

Derek got discharged from the Army in May of '72 and immediately began working, with great appreciation for the opportunity, as a chef at the Saloon. Uncle Joey's plan to retire was moving along faster than anticipated.

As planned, Regina and Derek wed in an intimate ceremony at the Lindy Docks. Thirty family and friends were in attendance, followed by a fun reception. After their honeymoon, they moved into Derek's family home and finally began their life together.

Their first year as newlyweds was great. Derek's cooking skills and business savvy rapidly improved. In June 1973, Regina graduated and decided to help Derek manage the business side of their restaurant. Derek's Uncle Joey and his wife officially turned the business over to the happy couple and moved to Florida in September. Derek and Regina sold the family home and moved into the Clamdiggers Saloon's spacious third-floor residence.

On October 16, 1973, Derek woke up and enjoyed a coffee out on the dock. On the crisp and clear morning, the bay was calm, and its surface looked like glass. He turned on a local radio station. "Good morning, New York, and happy Friday! It's hard to believe that today is the fourth anniversary of the Mets' epic upset of the Baltimore Orioles in 1969, and we're back in the Series again, tied one game each with the mighty Oakland A's."

Regina joined him, and he handed her a dozen red roses. "Happy first anniversary, Mrs. Williamson."

"Wow! You remembered our big day."

"Of course. That's why I picked the Mets' anniversary. I love you almost as much as I love them."

Regina punched his shoulder, and Derek playfully dropped to his knees. "Ouch!"

He then jumped up and asked, "Are you hungry?"

"Yes, I am, and I'd love one of your legendary breakfast bowls."

"Well, Mrs. Williamson, your wish is my command." At that moment, the song "Colour My World" by Chicago played, and Derek grabbed Regina's hand. They slow danced and kissed passionately.

The next few years were tremendous. Derek and Regina learned to manage the increasingly popular Clamdiggers Saloon. They also hired Freddie as a kitchen manager, and he flourished.

They established a manageable schedule that enabled them to be profitable and still have time to enjoy life. They especially loved Saturday evenings after closing time, where they'd prepare a couple of choice appetizers and break out a nice bottle of Chianti. When the weather permitted, nothing could beat eating, drinking, and listening to music out on the dock while taking in the bay's magnificence.

FATE

In the fall of 1978, Regina got pregnant with a due date of July 1979. The thrilled couple began to plan accordingly. Regina would step aside from the business for a while and focus on the baby. She experienced morning sickness, and ironically, so did Derek. Apparently, the old wives' tales about husbands experiencing early pregnancy symptoms along with their spouses were true. They joked about it, but Derek's nausea did not stop with Regina's. Though he said he was fine, Derek looked tired and pale and mentioned he had been experiencing periodic fevers and night sweats. Their family doctor ran some tests with no specific conclusion.

Generally, life over the next few months was good for Derek and Regina, but Derek's chronic fatigue and weight loss concerned them. Derek eventually went to the local Veterans Administration hospital and was diagnosed with deadly non-Hodgkin's lymphoma, likely caused by his exposure to Agent Orange. Unfortunately, it was already aggressively ripping through his body.

Throughout his ordeal, Derek put on a strong face. Thank God their business was in good hands, which enabled him to get treatments. Once a superior physical specimen, Derek was reduced to a frail state, using a wheelchair to get around. That never curbed his determination to support and love Regina during her pregnancy.

Regina focused on keeping Derek as comfortable as possible, so she hired a caretaker to help. Bruno Maggio was a gentle giant of mixed Samoan and African-American descent. Thanks to the elevator Uncle Joey installed, Bruno could easily take Derek outside to periodically sit on the dock.

One morning, Regina talked with Bruno as Derek sat outside, wrapped in a blanket, reading.

"How's he doing?"

Bruno replied, "He's mentally tough, but he can only stand for short periods. He walks a few times a day, but that's getting more challenging. By the way, he's reading the letters you sent him while he was in Nam."

"Really?" She went out and sat with Derek.

He smiled at her. "Hey, baby. I love you. The letters are amazing. I'm glad I waited."

"I'll just sit here quietly, drink my tea, and let you finish."

After completing the eleventh letter, Derek asked Regina to read the final one. She moved her chair next to Derek's wheelchair, and he shared his big blanket with her. They sat side-by-side looking out at the bay on that beautiful spring morning. Fighting through tears, Regina read out loud:

April 28, 1970
Dear Derek,

This is my last letter to you while you're serving in that hellhole. I pray every morning that you get out of there alive and healthy. I'm not sure why you haven't written back, but I'm sure you have your reasons. I still plan to see you when you return, and I plan to be with you, Derek—if you want to be with me, of course.

We've been through so much craziness. My family is coming around about us possibly being together, especially now that you're honorably serving in the Army. I don't know how fate works, and I'm not sure if God has designs on which boys are perfect for which girls. I just feel so right when I'm with you, and I know you feel the same about me. I absolutely love talking with you, eating with you, listening to music with you, drinking with you, watching Mets' games with you, making love with you, and (of course) slow dancing at the Clamdiggers Saloon with you.

Derek Williamson, just so you know, I want to be your wife, and I want to have babies with you. I realize I just went out on a limb, but that is how I feel. Please get home safe.

With much love,
Regina

Beaming at each other, they sat quietly. Derek broke the silence. "I love you. Mrs. Williamson. How are you feeling? How's our baby doing?"

A teary-eyed Regina just nodded with a sad smile.

At that point, Thomas Fitzgerald, a regular weekend performer, walked out on the dock with a coffee in his hand and his guitar strapped over his shoulder. "Do you mind if I join you?"

Derek raised his hands high as if he were in church, then smiled. "It's so good to see you, Thomas. Please play for me and my date."

"I'd love to, Derek."

Thomas played a beautiful version of Steven Stills's masterpiece, "Helplessly Hoping."

When he finished, Derek asked, "Can you play 'Unchained Melody?' I want to slow dance with my wife."

Removing his blanket, Derek tried to get up. Regina called for Bruno, who helped Derek stand. "May I have this dance, Regina?"

Still crying, she stood. With Bruno standing by to prevent a dying man and a pregnant woman from falling, they were able to slow dance at the Clamdiggers Saloon one last time. This time, however, Derek could feel Regina's physical strength and Regina could feel Derek's inner strength.

Afterwards, Bruno wheeled Derek upstairs to take a nap. On that peaceful May afternoon, Derek passed away in his sleep. Later that summer, Regina gave birth to a healthy and beautiful baby girl named Emily Mae Williamson.

THE END

Staring Down from the Edge of Life

THE "SENIOR CITIZEN HIPPIE"

As Christmas 2019 approached, Lukas Wagner was staring down from the edge of life. He glared at the handgun lying on the table to his left, next to a glass of Chianti and two thinly rolled joints. He lit one of the joints, then tasted his wine as Van Morrison tunes blanketed the room. On this snowy December evening, he was sitting comfortably in his recliner in his cozy Bethel, NY home, which he bought in 1967. The recliner was the final gift his late wife, Rachel, gave him last Christmas. She'd passed away two months ago after battling breast cancer.

Lukas yelled, "Alexa, I love you!"

Alexa, the music-making toy his daughter Annie gave him, also last Christmas, replied, "It's good to be appreciated."

As Lukas admired the fluffy white snow gracefully falling outside, his antique clock emitted six loud *cuckoos*. Six o'clock. Christmas, his favorite holiday, was two days away, and he was reflecting on Rachel's passing. Life with her was extraordinary, but since she died, it had been a living hell. All because of a lie that once seemed tame, but now felt like King Kong stomped on his soul. Bad thoughts raced through Lukas's mind; Chianti, weed, and music were his prescriptions.

Lukas was a tall, physically imposing man of seventy-two years with a gentle presence. His parents died when he was four, and he was adopted by a loving couple with no extended family. In 1965 at the age of seventeen, Lukas quit high school and enlisted in the Marines. The "conflict" in Vietnam had not yet escalated, so it seemed safe. After basic at Parris Island and some additional training, he went to Vietnam.

There, Fate threw him a curve, as he fought in the violent Battle of Ia Drang Valley. Nearly three hundred Americans were killed and hundreds more wounded, including Lukas, who suffered a shot in his groin. He healed physically, but that wound, combined with his nagging PTSD, left him emotionally broken. He finished his Marine service filing records at Camp Lejeune until his discharge in 1967. While there, he got a tattoo, an eagle with the U.S. Marines motto, *Semper Fidelis: Always Faithful.* In private, Lukas battled his PTSD by getting stoned and reflecting on what he had to do in Nam.

Lukas returned to Bethel and bought his home, which he and Rachel gradually expanded over the years to meet their family's needs: an infant playground, a jungle gym swing set, a swimming pool, a sled riding hill. Papa Lukas and Gramma Rachel's place represented joy for their daughter, their grandson, and, recently, their two great-grandchildren.

Lukas worked as a carpenter and eventually became a master craftsman. His carpentry skills, combined with his business acumen, helped him attain a comfortable level of wealth. After his discharge, he let his black hair grow long and kept it that way, although it was now silver-gray.

In spite of Lukas's current suicidal thoughts, he was a fun-loving guy who admired and respected women. He successfully attracted girls in high school, but after Nam and prior to meeting Rachel, he avoided women because he felt damaged.

In the summer of 1969, American culture and Lukas's hometown were on a fateful collision course with the *Woodstock Music & Art Fair*. After chaotic planning, the promoters negotiated with Max Yasgur to hold the concert on his dairy farm. They expected fifty thousand people, but about four hundred thousand hippies showed up—four miles from Lukas's home.

THE "GUARDIAN ANGEL"

Back in Lukas's current grim reality, he pondered how to relieve his torment and reunite with Rachel. There were two thick towels nearby he planned to place behind his head. Staring at his pistol, he considered the best bullet entry point.

A cell phone call from "Guardian Angel" startled him. It was Rachel's twin sister, Rose.

"Hey, Rose."

"Merry Christmas, buddy. Are you okay?"

"Yeah, thanks."

"Have you made holiday plans?"

"I talked with Robbie about visiting him, but I think I'll pass. This Annie thing has my brain fried."

"I understand, Lukas. Maybe we should tell her everything."

"No. Rachel was adamant."

"I understand. You've been through a lot, Lukas, and we know you're hurting."

"Rose, you're my guardian angel."

CHUCK

Shortly after that call, someone pounded on his front door.

"Who is it!?" Lukas shouted.

"Police! Open up!"

"Kiss my ass, Chuck."

As his best friend, Chuck, came to join him, Lukas tucked his gun under the towels. Chuck was jovial and tall with a stocky build and a shaved head. He had two tattoos, one on each arm: *Damn the torpedoes, full speed ahead!* which he got at eighteen on a drunken trip to New Orleans and a heart with Cupid's arrow through it inscribed, *Joannie.*

Pulling up a chair, Chuck took a hit on the joint, then grabbed a beer in the kitchen and returned. He stared at the barren area by Lukas's fireplace. "That's weird—no Christmas tree in *your* house. Those gifts in the kitchen are for Wendy and Trey, right?"

"Yeah, I picked up a few things, but I haven't had the energy to decorate. I'm sure Annie is discouraging Robbie and Kristina from visiting. She's still pissed off at me."

Annie was Lukas's forty-nine-year-old daughter. After Rachel passed away in October, they'd had a falling out. Annie's twenty-four-year-old son, Robbie, and his wife, Kristina, were caught in the middle. They had two children—Wendy, age four, and Trey, age two—and lived in Chester, an hour away.

Annie's husband, Frankie, had died in a car accident in February. It was horrible for everyone, but especially for Annie, who lost her husband and her mother in an eight-month span.

Chuck said, "Joannie reminded me that tomorrow is your first Christmas since Rachel's passing. Are you okay?"

"No, man, I'm a mess."

WOODSTOCK: RACHEL

Chuck and Lukas were eight when they met as Little Leaguers, and they shared a firm mutual trust since. They were opposites. Chuck was gregarious while Lukas was laid-back. Chuck wanted to enlist with Lukas in '65 but got a waiver. Later in '69, he accompanied Lukas to Woodstock, where they met their future wives, attending the concert without their parents' permission.

Chuck reminisced, "I remember the first time you saw Rachel. You were sitting on our blanket, stoned and drinking sangria from a pouch."

Rachel Morgan was from Long Island, part of a wealthy and image-conscious family. Rose still lived on Long Island. Their mother was a political science professor at NYU, and their father was an esteemed corporate lawyer. Rachel and Rose went to private Catholic schools from first grade until their high school graduation in June 1969—two months before Woodstock. Rachel was the rebel, and Rose was the obedient one.

The sisters planned to study Political Science at the State University of New York at Albany. Rachel had a few rocky high school relationships, so her parents handpicked her mate, Brook Richardson, but they felt Rose was capable of finding a man on her own.

Rachel's privileged upbringing came with comfort and security, but she didn't care for its appearance-based nature. She loved her parents for providing a wonderful existence but resented their controlling tendencies. Brook was an only child who was also born into wealth. In the summer of '69, he was a college junior, intellectually, athletically, and socially mediocre.

"Yeah, she was beautiful with her long brown hair and amazing blue eyes. She caught me gazing at her as Sebastian played 'Darlin' Be Home Soon.' I was freaked, but then she smiled at me." Lukas pointed his finger at Chuck. "And you didn't do bad either—Joannie's amazing!"

Lukas and Chuck were at Woodstock from the beginning on Friday, when Richie Havens kicked things off. After an exhausting overnight hitchhiking journey, Rachel and Joannie arrived on Saturday morning.

Chuck remarked, "It's a shame the girls didn't see much of it. I remember us taking them out of there while Mountain was playing 'Stormy Monday.' Thank God I had the balls to ask the ladies to join us."

Lukas replied, "No, shit. Who knew our future wives were teenage runaways?"

A RIFT IN THE FAMILY

Shifting back to the current reality, Chuck tried to guide Lukas from the darkness. "Is there anything we can do?"

"No, man. I wanted to tell Annie the truth, but that freaked Rachel, so I didn't. Then she blurted out part of it on her freaking deathbed. I don't think she intended to, but she was heavily medicated, and died two hours later. Annie's hurtful reaction blew me away."

A consoling Chuck responded, "She lost her husband and mother in a short time. Give her time, and you'll get back to a righteous place."

WOODSTOCK: RUNAWAYS

Mentally, they slid back into the music, sipping on their drinks and watching the snow falling outside. Once Lukas and Chuck connected with Rachel and Joannie at Woodstock, they had a fantastic time—partying and listening to historically great music. The fellas went to Woodstock with loaded backpacks: water Thermoses, wine pouches, snacks, and weed.

The girls started to panic because they had to get home the next day before their parents returned from vacation, so the fellas offered to get them out of there on their motorcycles. It was a wild four-mile ride to Lukas's home. After learning about the girls' situation, they offered to drive them home in the morning. Their parents were due to come back on Sunday afternoon, so they had ample time. They agreed to get a good night's sleep and leave early.

After showering and eating a meal, they hung out at Lukas's home. Lukas put on Dylan's new album, *Nashville Skyline,* which was mellow, enabling them to easily converse. Despite their gruff looks, the girls felt safe with Lukas and Chuck. Joannie and Chuck sat on the couch, while Rachel and Lukas sat on a cushy rug across the room.

Rachel passionately shared her story with a captivated Lukas. After a while, she sighed. "I'm sorry. All I did was whine about my bullshit. What about you, Lukas? What's your story?"

It was one-thirty in the morning.

"Not much to tell, but I'm certain I'm falling in love with you. Could I please kiss you?"

Rachel didn't say a word but gave him a welcoming look. Lukas slowly leaned forward and tenderly kissed Rachel for a few blissful minutes, then leaned back, relishing the experience. "We have an early start tomorrow. God, you're beautiful."

Rachel wished she could stay there forever.

The fellas set the girls up in the two bedrooms, and they slept on the couches.

A CONFRONTATION ON LONG ISLAND

After a good night's sleep and breakfast, they headed to Long Island in Chuck's VW van. They had an amazing time wearing out Chuck's eight-track player. The musical highlight of the drive was a hit song called "Polk Salad Annie." They played it several times and sang along.

An elated Rachel shouted, "If I have a daughter, I'm naming her Annie!"

They thought they arrived in time, but there was a police car in front of her house. In a bad twist of fate, their parents had returned home early. When their eighteen-year-old runaway daughters pulled up in a VW van with two elder hippies, they were frantic. The girls jumped out of the van and ran into the house. The young men leaned on the van as the girls' fathers confronted them.

Lukas calmly said, "We met the girls at Woodstock and offered to get them home safely—which we did, sir."

Both fathers did what looked like a choreographed 180 to confront the girls in the house. A cop then came over to interrogate Lukas and Chuck. After a brief discussion, he went inside to question the girls and returned.

"It looks like chivalry is not dead, gentlemen. Thanks for what you did." Lukas asked about the girls. "They have some explaining to do, but thanks to you they're safe." The cop noticed Lukas's *Semper Fidelis* tattoo. "Marine?"

"Marine and Vietnam vet. Ia Drang Valley in '65— the beginning."

The cop revealed a similar tattoo. "Operation Junction City in '67. *Semper fi,* brother." As they shook hands, the girls' parents came out, apologized to the guys, and thanked them.

The girls followed and gave emotional hugs.

Lukas told Rachel, "I'll be in touch. I meant what I said last night."

He kissed her on her forehead, then eased into the van.

THE PREGNANCY

The days after Woodstock were eventful. Chuck and Joannie connected and got to know each other. Under pressure to pursue her parents' goals, Rachel headed up to Albany with her sister a week later. Lukas passionately pursued Rachel during her first three weekends at school, a two-hour drive from Bethel. Though Rachel focused on her studies, being with Lukas dominated her thoughts, and she welcomed him every Saturday.

They got to know each other on a deep level. Eventually, they became intimate. Lukas felt revived, and Rachel hoped she could finally pursue happiness, but also started to feel nauseated. At that same time, Brook Richardson called Rachel to inform her he would visit on Friday.

"I don't want to see you, Brook. I'm not feeling well."

"I forgive you for the Woodstock thing. We had such a nice time together."

"You forgive me? Oh my God! We had a nice time? Don't come!"

Brook's pathological sense of entitlement angered Rachel, whose fourth weekend at Albany was intriguing. She and Lukas agreed he would drive over and take Rachel back to his place for a few days of relaxation.

When Lukas arrived, he saw Rachel sitting next to Brook on a bench. Rose burst through the exit door, aggressively walked toward them, and grabbed Brook by his shoulders. She shook him as she told him Rachel wasn't feeling well and to drive home *now*. As a dejected Brook departed, Lukas stayed out of sight. The girls sat quietly.

Lukas came to sit between them. "Is everything okay?" They simultaneously hugged Lukas, who joked, "Now *this* is the way to spend a Friday night."

They laughed, and Rachel said, "I'm so glad you came, Lukas."

"What's the deal with that Brook dude?"

Rose stood. "Rachel and I just ended any hopes he had of being with her. Please don't give that piece of shit another thought." Lukas stared in amazement, sensing something heady was happening. "I'll leave you two alone. It's been an intense week."

Rachel said, "Let's take a ride. I'm hungry and I have something important to tell you."

They went to Gracie's Café, and Lukas sat nervously fidgeting with his silverware while Rachel went to the bathroom. When she returned, he asked, "Did your parents tell you not to see me? That's not an option. I love you."

"Lukas, I'm pregnant! I'm having your baby!"

Lukas was dumbfounded. In a much-needed distraction, their waitress came over and took their orders. Lukas then excused himself to the men's room, splashed water on his face and reflected on this dilemma. As he wrestled with what to say, an inspiring wave of clarity engulfed him.

When he headed back, Rachel asked, "Are you angry?"

"I love you, Rachel. More than you can ever imagine."

They ate their meals in silence. As they finished, Lukas asked, "How serious is your relationship with Brook?"

Rachel broke into tears, then stormed into the ladies room where she stayed for about ten minutes. Crazy with worry, Lukas asked the waitress to check on her. Shortly after, the ladies came out, and Rachel thanked the waitress for the great advice. She then sat down and grabbed Lukas's hand. "Please promise me you won't freak out."

A confused Lukas replied, "What are you going to tell me?"

"God damnit, promise me, Lukas."

Lukas calmed down as Rachel explained, "My parents put enormous pressure on me to go out with Brook, so I went on three dates with him. I wasn't attracted to him, but I gave it a shot. At the end of the first night, he kissed my cheek and said goodnight.

"After the second date, we went to Town Pointe Park, where young people go to make out. We talked and then kissed for a few minutes. It felt forced, and his hands wandered, so I pushed back and politely asked to go home. He later asked me out for dinner the next weekend, right before Woodstock, and I agreed, with the intention of ending things.

"Brook drank several beers at dinner and convinced me to go back to Town Pointe 'to just talk.' I thanked him for a nice dinner and quickly told him I didn't want to see him again. He became frustrated and tried to kiss me again, and I refused. But that night, he forced himself on me, and I mentally went to another place. Afterwards, we each covered up, and he drove me home. It was awkward, and he acted like everything was normal. When we got to my house, he tried to kiss me goodnight. I left in a daze; I don't think he realized what he did."

Abruptly, Lukas stood up, rubbed his eyes, then ran his hand through his hair. "I'll kill him."

A tearful Rachel was adamant she didn't want anyone else to know what Brook did to her. She felt ashamed and blamed herself.

A more rational Lukas said, "I'm so sorry to hear that you went through that. Are you okay?"

"Yes, I'm dealing with it, and I don't want to stir up shit with our families. It's all a blur. I wore a pretty dress knowing we were going to a nice restaurant, and I tried to be cordial. Did I mislead him? I've been trying to block out the entire ordeal. Meeting you at Woodstock moved me in a positive direction."

Lukas nodded. "That makes me happy. First off, it's bullshit that you misled him. What he did was wrong. Rachel, it's important that you know something." Lukas then turned his head slightly and glanced out the window. He took a deep breath. "I'm sterile. My war wound did some internal damage, and I can never father a child. I'm so sorry to drop that on you, but you have to know, especially now."

Rachel murmured, "So I'm carrying Brook's baby."

"Actually, you're carrying *your* baby, and that is sacred. That piece of shit doesn't deserve you, and he doesn't deserve to be a father."

"What are you suggesting, Lukas?"

As the waitress refilled their cups, they talked about their dilemma. They vowed to work things out and decided Rachel could quit school and move in with Lukas. Lukas was getting his feet on the ground as a carpenter and owned a home.

"How will your parents react?" Reality was sinking in, and Lukas considered how they could live with this lie.

"I'll explain and offer to include them in our plans. It's up to them if they want to support us."

"What about Rose?" Lukas asked. "You have an incredible bond with her. Would this upset that?"

"Hell no, she has my back, and she respects you, Lukas. In fact, she told me today that she has a good feeling about you."

"Okay, let's sleep on it. I'll take you to your dorm, get a hotel, and pick you up for brunch tomorrow." He pointed at a sign promoting Gracie's Saturday brunch special. "Please invite Rose. I have something to do in the morning; I'll pick you up at noon."

The next day, Lukas arrived at twelve sharp, and they luckily got seated at the same waitress's table. They enjoyed an amazing meal, feeling upbeat. After they ate, Lukas pulled out a modest but beautiful engagement ring, which he'd bought that morning, and got down on one knee.

"Rachel, will you be my wife?"

"Yes, Lukas, I'd love to be your wife."

The waitress yelled, "Hey folks, they're getting married! How about a round of applause?"

That set off a loud standing ovation. This amazing love story and the accompanying ominous lie had just taken an interesting turn.

Rachel, Rose, and Lukas made a pact. They would never tell this baby three things: (1) the name of the biological father, (2) Rachel was a rape victim, and (3) Lukas had a traumatic war wound. They agreed to take this to their graves.

FAMILY LIFE

On the day prior to Christmas Eve 2019, the fellas were feeling good, and they were hungry. Chuck suggested they head to Francesca's for the holiday prime rib dinner.

"Dude, I'm way too scorched to drive, and it's snowing," Lukas said nervously.

"Joannie can drive us over, and we can get an Uber back. She has something going on later."

After a while, Joannie arrived. "Damn, you old geezers are smoking up a storm." She greeted Lukas, who got up and hugged her. "Are you okay, buddy?"

"I'm sorry, Joannie. I've been thinking about a lot of bad shit lately. I'm a wasted mess."

Turning her head to the side, she wiped tears from her eyes. "As you should be, my dear friend. You lost the love of your life, and you had a rift with your daughter, but Dr. Chuck has a cure—steak and adult beverages."

When they arrived at Francesca's, Joannie pulled Chuck aside. "Stay on Lukas like white on rice and help him get through this." A concerned Chuck hugged and kissed his amazing wife, and then the fellas went inside and devoured their much-needed prime ribs.

As their gargantuan dinners settled, the two old stoned-out hippies sat with shit-eating grins. They grabbed a table back in the bar and ordered a bottle of Chianti.

Chuck continued to reminisce. "It had to be tough asking Rachel's dad for permission to marry her."

"Yeah, we agreed the three of us should inform Rachel's parents about the pregnancy, then ask permission to get married. Thank God for Rose. She helped keep things calm. Her father initially flipped out, then yelled at Rachel about screwing up the arrangement with Brook."

"As I recall, Rachel's father was intense."

"Absolutely. Rose took him to another room for a while, and their mom sat with us. She was crying while staring at us with a big smile. Rose and her father came back, and he reluctantly said, 'You have my blessing, Lukas, but be kind to Rachel.' I assured him I would. That's when I decided Rose was my guardian angel."

Chuck refilled their glasses. "How are you feeling now?"

"Much better, thanks." Lukas had started the evening planning to join Rachel in the afterlife. Now, thinking of the good old days, he was actually enjoying himself.

After their wedding, Lukas and Rachel moved into Lukas's home and began life as a married couple with their secret held tightly. In April 1970, they had their beautiful baby girl, Annie, named after the song, "Polk Salad Annie." Rachel's mother and Rose visited often, and Rachel's father gradually came to understand Lukas—his upbringing and his values. He was also impressed with his business savvy. Additionally, Brook Richardson got arrested in the summer for inappropriately touching a young lady. Mr. Morgan realized he was wrong.

Chuck continued, "Then you both lost your parents."

"Yeah, tough times, man. Before we knew it, we were a functioning family. We loved the school stuff, soccer, Girl

Scouts, music lessons. Annie was the center of our universe, and she had no idea about our dreaded secret. Fuck!" Lukas pounded his fist on the table, and their waitress rushed over to check on them. They both quietly acknowledged all was well.

As the DJ played Springsteen's version of "Merry Christmas Baby," Chuck said, "You were great parents and played the hand you were dealt. Annie was a great kid. You know Joannie and I couldn't have kids, so we loved living vicariously through her. Then she had Robbie, and Robbie and Kristina had kids, and you became great-grandparents. Time really flew."

VISITORS

To Lukas's surprise, Joannie returned, and she was accompanied by Rose. "Wow, great to see you."

Rose responded, "We've been worried about you."

Lukas's cell phone interrupted; it was his grandson, Robbie. "Hey, Papa Lukas! Merry Christmas. I have an announcement. Kristina's pregnant."

Lukas plopped down in his chair. "Oh my God, that's wonderful."

Joannie and Rose joined the fellas for drinks, and a smiling Rose said, "It looks like you got the good news, buddy."

Chuck and Joannie convinced Lukas to spend the night at their place and, after a good night's sleep, drove him home. Around ten a.m. on Christmas Eve, they quietly pulled into the driveway of his seemingly empty home. "Surprise!"

A NOSTALGIC TOAST

Lukas's entire family was there and in full Christmas mode. Last night, Lukas's guardian angel led an effort to set everything up. His grandson, Robbie, handled Lukas's traditional Christmas Eve breakfast: waffles, eggs, hash brown potatoes, a fruit tray, whipped cream, and sausage from Tony Dee's Market in town. A fully decorated tree held gifts underneath, including the ones Lukas bought. In spite of his joy, Lukas noticed Annie's absence. He suppressed that thought and tried to relish the moment.

His great-grandchildren ran up and hugged him. "We love you, Papa Lukas. Merry Christmas!"

Overcome with emotion, Lukas burst into tears. He glanced over at the couch in a momentary panic, wondering where his revolver was, when Robbie brought him a plate of food.

"Here you go. I love you, Papa."

The swinging door from the kitchen then burst open. "Who wants a homemade cinnamon bun? I learned this amazing recipe from my papa, Mr. Lukas Wagner." A bewildered Lukas just stared at his beautiful daughter. She was aging gracefully, exactly like her mother had.

Walking over, Annie grabbed his hand. "Have a coffee with me, Papa."

Lukas followed her into the kitchen, and Annie gestured for him to sit at the table. She grabbed the coffee pot and stood over him, filling his cup. Then, while he waited for her to join him, Annie firmly slapped Lukas on the back of his head. "What the fuck, Papa! What were you planning to do with that gun? Don't you realize we love you?"

Lukas sighed, weak and vulnerable. "I desperately wanted to be with your mother. I haven't felt right since she passed. I was broken when I met her at Woodstock, and she fixed me. Then she left me, and I thought I lost you."

Annie sat down, then grabbed Lukas's hand and held it close to her heart. "You're like a superhero who swept Mom off her feet and rescued us. Yesterday, Aunt Rose broke your fifty-year-old vow and told me everything. Papa, I'm so sorry. I've been angry and resentful since Frankie died and all we went through with Mom. Then the news that you're not my biological father. I took out my anger on you. In my defense, I didn't know about the violence you experienced in Vietnam and your terrible injury.

"I didn't know about my piece-of-shit biological father. I didn't know about your willingness to raise her daughter who wasn't biologically yours. I knew you loved Mom, but that is amazing. I acted like an impetuous teenager. Please, forgive me." Annie hugged Lukas.

Pulling away, Lukas looked into Annie's eyes. "I was there when you arrived. I changed your diapers. I watched you crawl and eventually get up and walk. I taught you how to ride a bike. I went to your recitals and sporting events. I comforted you when you were scared, and I did my best to intimidate the boys who pursued you."

"Yes, you did. I remember when you sat on the front porch on a date night, wearing military camouflage pants, a torn t-shirt, and a ragged John Deere hat. You poured iced tea into an empty Jack Daniels bottle and pretended you were cleaning a broken shotgun. That boy was scared to death after you had your 'talk' with him while slugging a long sip from the bottle."

Lukas shrugged his shoulders, smiled, and continued, "I was at your high school and college graduations. I was thrilled to dance the bride/father dance at your wedding—of course to your song, 'Polk Salad Annie.' We blew them away, kiddo! My God, you've been through so much."

Feeling relieved and oddly satisfied, Lukas took a deep breath and affectionally smiled at his daughter as he rubbed his chin. With holiday music playing in the background, Robbie walked in. "Please join us for the gifts exchange. The kids are going crazy."

Standing around the beautiful Christmas tree were all the people Lukas loved.

Annie announced, "Grab your beverage: coffee, orange juice, water, or one of those great mimosas Aunt Rose made." She held up her glass. "A toast. To an honorable man, a Vietnam vet, a successful businessman, my father and my hero, Lukas Wagner."

Everyone toasted, then gave Lukas a round of applause. Lukas's four-year-old great-granddaughter, Wendy, ran up to him. "Are you really a hero, Papa Lukas?"

A huge smile blooming on his face, he picked her up and kissed her. At her age, he'd lost his parents. How fortunate he was to be a part of Wendy's life.

Annie joined them, wrapping an arm around her father's waist. "Yes, Wendy. Papa Lukas is a superhero."

Chuck then shouted, "Speech! Speech!"

With a deep breath, Lukas regained his composure. "Thank you—all of you—for this beautiful gathering. To my beautiful Rachel, we miss you dearly. And to everyone here, 2019 has been a difficult year, but I'm confident 2020 will be a memorable one."

THE END

From the Frying Pan

THE CREW

On a memorable Friday evening in 1982, Jimmy B's Italian Ristorante buzzed with people, food, and music. The elegant and comfortable Long Island eatery attracted huge weekend crowds. The owner, Jimmy Bonano, was a distinguished-looking man in his sixties with silver-gray hair who wore expensive, well-tailored suits.

"Good evening, gentlemen," Jimmy stated.

Gaeth O'Neil, Johnnie Murphy, and CB, three close friends known as "The Crew," respectfully stood and shook Jimmy's hand. After his wife, Rosa, passed away several years ago, Jimmy became a charismatic figurehead at the restaurant, and his son, Vincent, and daughter-in-law, Anna, took over the reins.

The Crew came to Jimmy B's on Friday nights and were among the select few in Jimmy B's "circle," primarily made up of Italians with family or business connections. To maintain contact, Jimmy provided a standing Friday night reservation for The Crew, telling Gaeth it was in appreciation of his service in Vietnam. None of them knew the truth, and Jimmy had promised Gaeth's mother they never would.

VIETNAM VET VERSUS SILVER SPOONER

Gaeth was a Vietnam veteran and The Crew's informal leader. He was average-looking, but beyond belief in his essence and charisma. People were easily drawn to him. The name Gaeth was Old Irish and meant "intelligent and skillful." Gaeth's father, a festive Irish immigrant and incessant woman-izer, had named him, the only thing Gaeth appreciated about him. Gaeth was an infant when a jealous husband pushed his father in front of a train to his death. That incident later embarrassed Gaeth, who *was* in fact smart and skillful, but also sensitive and emotional. Since his discharge from the Marines, he drew a VA disability check and did odd construction jobs. Gaeth got married, but that failed.

After conversing with The Crew, Jimmy excused himself to head home. As they said farewell, Jimmy's boisterous son, Vincent, was yelling in the kitchen. A disgusted Jimmy shook his head. Vincent was your typical silver-spooner: tall, dark, and handsome with a favorable genetic and financial chain, making his youth a breeze. When a potential relationship represented personal gain, he was charming. Otherwise, he was a selfish prick.

THE FRYING PAN INCIDENT

Bernie, the waitress, took The Crew's orders: CB, spaghetti and meatballs; Johnnie, linguine with red clam sauce; and Gaeth, a bowl of minestrone. As various crooners sang in the background, they savored their wine. CB's spaghetti arrived with sausage instead of meatballs, and he loudly complained to Bernie.

The food at Jimmy B's was excellent, but Gaeth was there to observe Anna. Gaeth loved the way she looked, the way she smiled, and the way she glided through the restaurant. In high school, Gaeth and Anna came close to going on a date, but her father sternly objected to a relationship with a guy with no future. Unfortunately for Gaeth, she would later marry Vincent in an arranged match. Fate would not rest, as yet another unfortunate incident loomed.

Vincent happened to be walking past The Crew's table as CB complained loudly, "Hey, I ordered meatballs! Why did I get sausage?"

"I don't care what you ordered. Eat it the way it is, Space Man," Vincent reacted.

"I like meatballs, asshole!" CB yelled.

Vincent's face reddened, reflecting his disdain for The Crew, and Bernie admonished him, "Be nice, Vincent."

Gaeth and Vincent locked eyes; their fragile levee was about to burst.

Back in the kitchen, Vincent screamed at Bernie, "Don't contradict me, especially in front of those dickheads. That idiot can barely tie his shoes!"

The Crew was in earshot, the fateful last straw.

Gaeth stood up, winked, and told CB, "I got this, champ."

CB responded, "I think I ran over another dog today, Gaeth."

"No, champ, you missed him." Gaeth, as he often did, steered CB away from the thought of killing dogs. CB was six-feet-three-inches tall with bright red hair, and he talked loudly with a big smile, which caused him to stand out. Once, Gaeth affectionately described CB as "not completely with the program." CB was physically strong and an incredibly loveable guy.

CB's Grandpa Patrick, an aging and frail gentleman, raised CB after his parents died. CB's actual name was Culhan Byrne, a variant of Cu Chulainn. Irish legend had it that he served the chief Culann in payment for killing his dog. Oddly enough, a while back, CB accidentally ran over a dog with his pickup truck, which broke his heart and caused his fixation.

With CB calmed, Gaeth entered the kitchen, intending to politely ask Vincent to apologize.

As Gaeth walked toward him, Vincent yelled, "What the fuck are you doing?" Vincent stormed toward Gaeth, pointed at him, and accidentally poked his nose. Gaeth's restraint vanished. He grabbed a small cast iron frying pan and swatted Vincent upside the head with a swift backhand, knocking him out.

The normally sedate eatery bustled with commotion as two siren-screaming vehicles arrived. The medics rushed Vincent off in an ambulance, and the police took Gaeth away in handcuffs. Gaeth shouted to Johnnie to call Grandpa Patrick to let him know CB was okay.

THE GROOM-TO-BE

As the commotion at Jimmy B's subsided, CB ate his corrected meal while Johnnie sipped on his Chianti. Gaeth was going to jail, and their cherished Friday-night ritual was in jeopardy. Obeying Gaeth's instructions, Johnnie called Grandpa Patrick and explained the fiasco.

He responded, "I've always liked Gaeth. He's special. Too bad things got violent."

At eighty-nine, Grandpa Patrick was in failing health and worried about CB's fate. They were in bad financial shape and lived in a dilapidated house. CB would need lifelong support, and Grandpa Patrick was banking on Gaeth's and Johnnie's kindness when his time came.

Johnnie, a gregarious and hard-working guy, was a descendant of Irish immigrants. People loved to be around him because he had a way of making them feel good. Johnnie was about to marry his girlfriend, Colleen, in two weeks.

Johnnie's humble but welcoming home was the social center for those close to him, especially Colleen, The Crew, and Grandpa Patrick. They were basically a dysfunctional but supportive family unit. Gaeth and CB were in the wedding party, and Jimmy, Vincent, and Anna would attend.

A CONFLICTED FRIEND

Anna and Johnnie sustained a close friendship, beginning in high school when they attended classes together. Johnnie made her laugh, and she loved his company. He was also Gaeth's best friend, which appealed to her. Their unique and enduring friendship strengthened further when The Crew started coming to Jimmy B's on Friday nights. Their friendship, however, was always conflicted due to the tension between Gaeth and Vincent.

Anna was a strikingly beautiful woman with a classic Italian look—gorgeous black hair and a dark, smooth complexion. She was petite with captivating hazel eyes reeking of sincerity and sensuality. When Anna walked by, men were compelled to look and admire her. As a young woman, her well-intentioned but overbearing father overwhelmed her. Her parents divorced when she was a child, resulting in several "no-win" conflicts. In high school, Anna was attracted to Gaeth and would periodically stroll home with him. Anna loved those walks.

Being with Gaeth felt natural, but their walks ended over one simple word. During their final trip together, Gaeth worked up his nerve and told her he liked her.

She asked why, and he said, "Because you're the prettiest girl in town, and you're quirky."

Thinking he meant she was ditzy, she got upset. Anna saw herself as assertive and intelligent, not quirky. Gaeth unsuccessfully tried to explain, but Anna stayed mad at Gaeth for too long.

Shortly after high school, when Anna was first engaged to Vincent, she crossed paths with Gaeth when he was about to go to Vietnam. He candidly told her not to marry Vincent. "Because people will make fun of your new name—Anna Bonano."

They conversed briefly, and he departed feeling sad. Things were moving too fast for Anna, and she yearned to talk with Gaeth, but she wouldn't see him again until he returned from his tour of duty.

SECOND FRIDAY NIGHT—THE DRUNK AND THE KISS

One week after the frying-pan incident, Sinatra's classic "Summer Wind" played at Jimmy B's as customers ate, drank, and talked. Johnnie and CB were in attendance, but Gaeth was still in jail.

Johnnie and Grandpa Patrick tried to bail him out, but he said, "Fuck it. I'll hang out and think things through."

As Johnnie and CB sipped on their Chianti, Anna joined them and inquired about Gaeth.

Johnnie explained about Gaeth's stubbornness. "We wish Vincent wasn't pressing charges, but we understand. By the way, how's he doing?"

"He'll be okay soon," Anna responded. "Johnnie, I recently heard you and Gaeth talking about handling Grandpa Patrick's funeral when his time comes. Is everything okay with that?"

"Gaeth told me he'd figure it out. You know him. He always gets things done, and I'll certainly do my part. Are you and Vincent still coming to the wedding?"

Anna smiled. "We'll be there, Johnnie."

TIME FOR REFLECTION

Meanwhile, Gaeth's week in jail was therapeutic. He sat in his cell reading *The Catcher in the Rye*, reflectively working his way through that powerful story. He felt sympatico with Holden Caulfield's peculiarities, particularly his disdain for phony people. Evaluating his life, he was surprisingly good with everything. He did decide to stop going to Jimmy B's on Friday nights and find another place, hopefully with Johnnie and CB.

He met Rex, an elderly man charged with drunk and disorderly, in an adjoining cell.

Rex proudly told Gaeth, "I'm an out-of-work song-and-dance man."

After a litany of Rex's stories, Gaeth demanded, "Show me what you got, old man."

Rex leaped right into an incredible song-and-dance version of "Me and My Shadow."

A shocked Gaeth applauded. "Who the fuck *are* you? Mr. Bojangles?"

"Actually, that song was based on my life," Rex boasted, and Gaeth just smiled.

They talked a while longer about music, life, and love. Rex told Gaeth he was certain people had the ability to fall in love many times.

Standing up with a gleam in his eyes, he pounded his chest. "Look at me! I've been in love with a bunch of 'em! And I'm certain they'll all come to my funeral."

Lying on his cell bunk, Gaeth replied with disgust, "I'd be lucky to get more than a few close friends to show up at mine. Good night, Rex."

That was the last time Gaeth saw Rex, as his son bailed him out while Gaeth was sleeping.

A while later, an officer unlocked Gaeth's cell door. "A lady's here to bail you out, and no isn't an option. We're tired of looking at your sorry ass."

Gaeth assumed his ex-wife got word and came to his rescue. Although embarrassed, he thought seeing her would be nice. He headed to the men's room and stared at the mirror with blinding focus. *What have I become? I'm obsessed with a woman I can never have. I assaulted her husband, and now my ex-wife is stuck cleaning up my mistakes.*

As he exited, he turned left and heard the ladies room door slam shut behind him.

A distinct voice said, "Hello, Gaeth."

It was Anna.

A shocked Gaeth asked, "What's going on?"

"Johnnie told us you were being stubborn; Jimmy sent me to make things right."

Overwhelmed with emotion, Gaeth looked at Anna's captivating face, instinctively pulled her next to him, and held her. They briefly stood there hugging; then Gaeth gently kissed her forehead. He poured years of pent-up affection into those few tender moments. For the first time in years, Anna felt like a woman, a beautiful and appreciated woman. Gaeth placed his palms on each of her soft cheeks, looked into her eyes, and kissed her gently on her lips. He completely appreciated this fleeting opportunity like a rare delicacy, then walked away. It was unspoken, but mutually understood: they could go no further with their desire.

THIRD FRIDAY NIGHT—THE WEDDING

Johnnie's wedding took place on a Friday evening at a resort-style hotel on Long Island's North Shore. It was one week after Anna bailed Gaeth out of jail, and two weeks after Gaeth smashed an iron frying pan upside Vincent's thick skull. Most of the people who attended stayed at the hotel and enjoyed a festive event with great food, music, drinking, and dancing. Vincent, there with Anna and Jimmy, drank early and got bombed. A few of Jimmy's guys took Vincent to his room to sleep it off, leaving Anna unaccompanied.

The DJ announced it was time for the Best Man toast. With a glass of champagne in hand, Gaeth stood at the head table and quickly scanned the audience of about 150 smiling people, all thoroughly enjoying the festivities. Gaeth nervously took a deep breath, then asked everyone to charge their glasses and stand.

"Johnnie and Colleen, we love you. It's a cruel world, and you need to relentlessly care for each other. You're *so* lucky to have found each other. If you ever need anything from me, say the word. I got your back! Please be kind to each other and love each other without fail. God bless you. Cheers!"

Glasses clanked and people laughed as they responded, "Cheers!"

As the audience cheered and applauded, Gaeth headed to the bar and ordered a Chianti. The DJ started the dinner music with a choice selection, Sinatra's "Fly Me to the Moon." At that point, Anna strolled toward Gaeth, and he was awed. She was wearing a plain black dress, high heels, and a white pearl necklace. With all of the recent upheaval, Anna didn't put much effort into her wedding preparation, but in Gaeth's eyes, she looked breathtaking. She leaned up against the bar right next to him, and he took in her fragrance, thoroughly admiring her beautiful face.

"Nice toast there, Mr. Best Man."

"Thanks. Where's Neanderthal Man?"

"Down for the count. He's been under a lot of pressure with work stuff combined with you hitting him in the head."

"I'd tell you I'm sorry, but I'm not. More importantly, you look beautiful, Anna. Would you like a drink?"

"I damned sure would, cowboy."

Anna's uncharacteristically loose response made Gaeth nervous. They talked for a few minutes, and Gaeth told Anna, "Thanks again for bailing me out. You didn't have to do that."

"It was Jimmy's call, and I was happy to help. I couldn't let our boy Johnnie get married without a best man. I know Vincent was rude to CB and how protective of him you are. Vincent realizes he messed up, and I convinced him not to press charges."

"Anna, are we cool with what happened at the police station?"

"You tell me, Gaeth," Anna responded seductively.

"I gotta get out of here. You look *so* good. Enjoy the wedding." Frazzled, Gaeth set down his drink and left.

He headed to his hotel room, removed his tuxedo jacket and tie, then opened his emergency bottle of Chianti. Sipping on his wine, he sat alone, when he heard a knock. He opened the door, and there stood Anna.

"Can I come in?"

"That's not a good idea. What about Vincent and Jimmy?"

"Vincent's done for the night. Tequila got him. And Jimmy's busy flirting with a few older ladies."

Anna eased inside, and Gaeth poured her a glass of wine. After they sat silently for a time, Anna purposefully stood up, faced Gaeth, and began to slowly unzip the back of her black dress.

"What are you doing?"

"I want you to see what I look like naked, Gaeth."

"I already know. I've visualized you often. I feel like I know every detail of your face, your neck, your shoulders, your breasts, the curve of your back."

"Don't you want to make love to me?"

"I *don't* want to cause you to violate your vows. I violated mine more than I care to mention. We'll feel better if we keep it above the shoulders." Speaking with amazing clarity, Gaeth walked up to Anna. He tenderly kissed her, and she loved how he made her feel. She closed her eyes and melted into this incredibly surreal moment.

About to go out of his mind, Gaeth stepped back and walked in circles. He regained his composure, sat in his chair, and looked at Anna, sitting on the bed.

They shared their stories. Gaeth spoke of Vietnam, his failures, his ex-wife, and his unfortunate use of the word "quirky."

"What happened to you, Gaeth? Was it Vietnam?"

"I don't know! It was so many things. It was pissing you off. It was not having the balls to talk you out of marrying Vincent. It was your father putting me down. It was Nam. I don't know!"

"Did you say you were going to stop me from marrying Vincent?"

"Don't you remember when I told you not to marry him?"

"Yes, but you were joking around about my new name, Anna Bonano."

"The fact is I went there to try to convince you to change your mind. But when I saw you, I realized I couldn't give you what you deserved, a secure and normal life. So, I made a stupid joke and left disappointed."

Anna talked about her life—her good and bad choices. She assured Gaeth she found happiness in her children, and Jimmy was kind to her and kept Vincent in check.

"That's pretty fucking sad if you ask me!" After that awkward comment, they sat in silence for what seemed like an eternity. "You know I love you, Anna, but we weren't meant to be together."

Anna sadly smiled, then closed her eyes.

CUBANS AND CHIANTI

Gaeth woke up the next morning, and Anna was gone. Still wearing his disheveled tuxedo, he cleaned up, then grabbed the half-empty bottle of Chianti and three Cuban cigars from the bedstand. He headed outside of his first-floor room to relax in one of the chairs facing the hotel's interior courtyard.

Nothing like a cigar and Chianti at eight a.m.

The door next to his room burst open.

"Hey, Gaeth," CB called out. "Johnnie's coming over before he leaves for Cancun!"

"Eccellente!" Gaeth said with amusement. "How'd ya sleep, champ?"

"I had another dream about killing a dog."

"Did you run him over again?"

"I sure did."

"Don't worry about it, champ. The dog was rabid."

"What is rabid, Gaeth?"

"Vincent Bonano is rabid."

Johnnie then arrived. "You disappeared on me last night after your toast. Are you okay?"

"Yeah, I'm fine. I just needed to be alone."

As The Crew enjoyed a morning drink and cigars, Vincent and Anna exited their room across the courtyard. Vincent slowly walked by, carrying their overnight bags, and Anna followed a few feet behind. Vincent looked across at Gaeth and slightly bowed his head to acknowledge him. Gaeth responded with a similar nod. As she passed, Anna smiled at Gaeth, and he smiled back.

"God, I love to watch her walk," Gaeth said.

"Miss Anna's pretty!" CB blurted.

"She's the prettiest girl in town," Gaeth responded.

Attempting to change the subject, Johnnie asked Gaeth, "So, are you coming back to Jimmy B's on Friday nights, Gaeth?"

Proudly sporting his Chianti and Cuban cigar, Gaeth replied, "Nope. I'm going to start going to an Irish pub called Mac's Place. They serve an amazing beef stew."

CB asked, "Do I like beef stew, Gaeth?"

"I don't know, champ. You should get Johnnie and meet me there some Friday night. I hear it's better than spaghetti and meatballs."

CB sadly responded, "I should have eaten the sausage."

Johnnie jumped in. "Bullshit, CB! A change will do us good! You ordered fucking meatballs that night, and you deserved fucking meatballs! Besides, we won't have to deal with that asshole, Vincent, anymore."

CB concluded, "That's true, but now Gaeth won't get to see Miss Anna."

Gaeth stared up at the sky with a tear running down his cheek. After that fateful glance, Gaeth never saw Anna again.

THE EULOGY AND THE SECRET

Once The Crew agreed to a new tradition, they did their final toast. Johnnie went on his honeymoon. Over the next few months, things eased back to a relatively normal state. Mac's Place worked out fine, and Gaeth tried hard to forget Anna.

One Friday night, Gaeth was leaving Mac's Place after a great meal and several glasses of wine with Johnnie and CB. He walked toward his vehicle and approached a commotion in the parking lot. Three thugs, hyped up on drugs, were about to rob two young ladies Gaeth earlier saw sitting at the bar. After Gaeth politely attempted to get them to move on, one of them fired three shots at him, and he fell unceremoniously to the ground.

Despite Gaeth's dry comment to Rex during his stay in jail, the Irish wake for Gaeth at O'Brady's Funeral Home was a packed house. Everyone was still in shock over Gaeth's demise. As the crowd settled in, Jimmy B discreetly entered the main office of O'Brady's Funeral Home. He sat with his trusted friend, the funeral director, Robert O'Brady. They reviewed two piles of paperwork, and Jimmy signed two checks.

"This is very kind, Jimmy. Mr. O'Neil and eventually Mr. Byrne will both have fine funerals thanks to you," Robert O'Brady said respectfully.

"Thank you and please keep this between us. Nobody is to know about this. *Capisci?*" Jimmy began to cry.

Robert O'Brady asked, "Are you okay?"

Jimmy revealed the secret he maintained for over thirty years. "I'm over sixty years old, and I fathered two sons. Vincent was legitimate, and Gaeth was not, by society's standards. I never told Gaeth, and now he's gone."

Anna quietly entered. "Excuse me, gentlemen. Is everything okay?"

"Ah yeah, it's fine." Jimmy wiped his eyes, stood, and shook Robert O'Brady's hand. "Let's go pay our respects, Anna."

Four people spoke during the eulogy, and each fought through intense emotion in an inspiring celebration of Gaeth's life.

One of the surviving girls at Mac's Place said, "Thank you, Mr. O'Neil, for saving our lives. You came out of nowhere, smiled, and calmly asked them to do the right thing. 'No harm, no foul,' you said. You told the one with the gun that you were in Vietnam and that violence was senseless. You opened up your wallet and offered all your cash. When you handed them your money, we safely eased toward Mac's Place. As we did, you gave them your car keys and told them they could have it too. 'Let's walk away peacefully.' Then we heard the shots. I'm so glad you came by, but I hate that you're gone. Thank you, Mr. O'Neil, and God bless you. You saved our lives." She walked off weeping uncontrollably.

CB went next. "I'm so sad that Gaeth died. He was my best bud, and I loved him. I loved it when he called me champ. It's my fault. I should have ate the sausage. Then we would never have moved away from Miss Anna's place. Sorry, Gaeth."

After hugging CB, Johnnie stepped to the podium. "Nice job, CB. It's not your fault. There are evil people out there, and Gaeth ran into a few of them. He was the ultimate friend. I'm gonna especially miss our Friday night ritual: food, beverages, music, and feeling, as Gaeth would say, 'on top of the world.' When you were down, he had your back. It's terrible that this happened, but when I think about him, I'm going to smile. He was the leader of our Crew, a veteran who served honorably, and a great guy. Don't worry, Gaeth. I'll take care of CB. God bless you, amigo."

The last speaker was Grandpa Patrick. Johnnie helped him get to the podium because he was so frail. Speaking in his heavy Irish brogue, he said, "This young man was a prince. I can't thank him enough for looking out for CB the way he did. And thank you, Johnnie, for stepping up. Some people think that Gaeth wasn't the same when he got back from Vietnam. Hell, I don't know what happened over there. He never would talk about it. Gaeth once told me he made his own choices. His life may not seem productive to many, but he had a helluva good time. Sure, he cursed and drank a bit, but Gaeth O'Neil was a noble lad. I also know those close to him think he never really had a true love, but I know he did. He told me about it one night after having a few too many of those Chiantis he liked to drink. He was tortured by it every day, but as God is my witness, this young man loved a woman with all his heart and all his might. God bless you. We're going to miss you, old friend."

Anna sat between her husband and her father-in-law in the back of the room. Tightly clutching Jimmy's and Vincent's hands, she wept throughout the eulogy.

NOURISHMENT AT JIMMY B'S

After the evening eulogy, the Bonano family invited close friends and family to their restaurant. In addition to doing the right thing, this was Jimmy's way of welcoming back Johnnie and CB.

Jimmy said, "I may be Italian, but I know what it takes to have an appropriate Irish wake. Please come to our place for drinks and nourishment. Let's celebrate the life of this fine young man, this hero, Gaeth O'Neil."

It was a great night and perfectly suited for Gaeth. The Bonanos, with the help of Johnnie, took great care in placing a collage of photos of Gaeth's life on The Crew's table. Anna checked out the photos, which proved to be emotional. In addition to various shots from his life, two stood out. The first was a picture of Gaeth, Johnnie, and CB sitting at their table toasting the good times. Jimmy B stood behind them, and Gaeth's magnetic smile said, "All is right in the universe." The other notable photo was of The Crew again. This time, Anna was perched on Johnnie's lap, laughing uncontrollably. Anna had seen the snapshot before, but never really noticed Gaeth gazing at her with conspicuous admiration. Smiling, she shed a happy tear.

Throughout the evening, everyone ate, drank, and shared heartwarming stories about Gaeth. Although far from perfect, he was a good man, loved by many, and his life ended on a noble note. The night wrapped up, and the guests departed. Vincent Bonano left early to take care of their children, and Anna and Jimmy stayed behind to clean up. When they finished, they poured some red wine and relaxed.

After a few minutes of silence, Anna said, "I heard what you told Mr. O'Brady today."

Jimmy was speechless, and his hands trembled.

"I gave Teri O'Neil my word. I told her Gaeth would never know he was born out of wedlock. I gave her my word!" He pounded his fist on the table.

Startled, Anna listened compassionately as he continued his cathartic rant.

"I was in love with her. Yes, I was married, and I was also very much in love with Rosa. It just happened. Teri and I knew it was wrong. When she got pregnant, we concealed it from her husband and my Rosa. Her husband died shortly after Gaeth was born. I took care of her and the child financially, but Teri made me swear on a Bible that I'd never tell Gaeth. I agreed, but I also committed to doing what I could to help him. His Irish stubbornness made that difficult, but I tried. That's why I gave him a table every Friday night. After they quit coming to the restaurant, I paid his house off and had my lawyers disguise it as an inheritance from his deceased father. I was his father. He was my son."

He closed his eyes, then looked at Anna with a haunting, sorrow-filled expression. "It's utterly painful to be so passionately in love with someone, but not be able to pursue it. Do you understand what I'm saying, Anna?"

Anna tearfully responded, "I know, Jimmy. We're burying a good man tomorrow."

BURYING A GOOD MAN

The next day at the VA Cemetery, the same large crowd showed up to pay respects to Gaeth. The Marine Honor Guard marched up and took their positions. Father O'Leary said a few words about how Gaeth was a good Catholic boy even though he hadn't been to church lately. He joked that he probably could have used a good confession, but he was sure God would understand, knowing the kind of man Gaeth was and the rough go he had of it. He went on to talk about his service to our great country, his final brave act, and how he experienced true friendship.

He concluded by saying, "God bless you, Gaeth O'Neil."

Seven rifles simultaneously barked off piercingly loud shots, three times, startling Anna. As the Marines marched off, Anna grabbed a flower, got in line, and placed it on Gaeth's coffin, wondering what might have been.

Gaeth's tombstone read:

GAETH O'NEIL
Marine Friend Hero
Leader of "The Crew"
1952 – 1983

THE END

An Uncomfortable Destiny

A COLD AND LONELY NIGHT (SATURDAY 9:00 P.M.)

A howling wind blew powdery white snow in random circles outside of Gus's Place, a cozy Long Island pub. Inside, two lone patrons sat at the bar, entranced by the soothing fire dancing in the fireplace across the room. Gus, the owner and bartender, was an elderly gentleman of sixty-seven years.

On that life-changing Saturday evening in November 2006, anyone with sense stayed home, but these two people came to temporarily avoid their bitter realities.

The woman, Katherine, in her early forties, had a unique face, simultaneously reflecting the rigors of her life's journey and her appealing beauty. She wore faded jeans, an old, hooded sweatshirt and, incredibly on this frigid night, bedroom slippers. She hunched over the bar with the hood placed over her head, revealing the ends of her shoulder-length sandy hair and her lovely, but life-worn, face. Soft brown eyes displayed an external sense of comfort, but a closer internal look exposed a troubled but determined soul. Her life was a predictable pattern of hope followed by disenchantment, and men were her downfall.

The man sitting to Katherine's left, Karl, was an extremely big fellow in his late forties. He stood at about six feet, six inches and weighed over three hundred pounds. His head was shaved, and he sported an unruly goatee. Despite his intimidating size, he had a comforting presence and rarely experienced confrontation.

The various great songs pouring out from the jukebox provided a pleasant distraction, but a haunting silence crept into the bar when the machine exhausted all previous requests. Gus grabbed a handful of quarters from the cash register and laboriously plodded over to reload it.

"Any requests?" he yelled.

"Yeah," shouted Katherine. "Please play 'I Will Remember You' by Sarah McLachlan. I love that song. It's sad, and it makes me feel good."

Staring at the fire, Karl took a long, slow sip of his beer, wondering how a sad song could make Katherine feel good.

THE VULGAR INTRUDER (SATURDAY 9:45 P.M.)

As Katherine and Karl sat peacefully, Gus headed back to the storage room, but *boom!* The front door slammed shut as a man barged in. "Damn! It's fucking cold out there!"

Katherine and Karl glared at this peculiar individual as if he violated some sacred religious ritual by failing to bow his head or make a sign of the cross as he rudely entered their sacred institution, barking out vulgarities. He was conspicuously small with flaming red hair, like a pissed-off, modern-day leprechaun. He carefully scanned the bar and absorbed its essence. Clearly, his fifty-six years of life had prepared him for this evening of destiny. His demeanor said, "Bite me, bitch."

He strolled to the bar, sat two stools to Katherine's right, then slammed his fist. "How about a goddamn glass of Chianti?"

Rushing back, Gus happily shouted, "Brian McNerney, you crazy bastard! It's great to see you."

"Great to see you too, amigo," Brian responded.

"It's been a while, Brian."

"It has. Now how about you quit jerking me off, old man, and bring me my fucking wine?"

"Do you have to curse so much?" an annoyed Katherine barked at Brian. She hated that this obnoxious little man barged into her intimate place of refuge.

"Yes, I do have to curse. We live in America with freedom of speech. I fought for this country, and I'll curse if I want to." Brian then leaned really close to Katherine's face, stared at her, and slowly enunciated, "I love to curse. I'm a vulgarity virtuoso."

"Settle down, tough guy. We're just trying to relax and have a few drinks. Watch your language around the lady," Karl responded.

Brian boldly pointed a finger at Karl. "Chill out, you oversized piece of shit. I'm gonna take a piss, and when I return, I'll show you the true meaning of pain." Brian then stormed to the men's room.

Karl was shocked at this diminutive man's audacity.

Gus cautioned Karl, "Leave it alone, man. He's insane. Don't let his small size fool you. He's a Vietnam vet with a high threshold for pain. A few years ago, he beat a man to death with his toaster after the guy broke into his home. Legend has it he still uses that toaster because it cooks his bagels to perfection."

"For real?" Karl reacted.

"That's crazy!" Katherine agreed. "I'd never eat from a toaster used to kill someone."

"He's actually a great guy, but he can be completely whacked. Please don't mess with him. I don't need any bullshit in here."

Returning to the bar, Brian glared at Karl as he sipped his wine. The dilapidated jukebox helped ease the tension as Frankie Valli's "My Eyes Adored You" gracefully flowed from it. Brian glanced at Katherine and noticed the hidden beauty of her face under her hooded sweatshirt. What was she doing with Karl, the oversized lumberjack-looking dude, who apparently lacked a pair of balls? Brian was a foot shorter and about 150 pounds lighter. When he challenged Karl to go mano-a-mano, he received no response.

HOSTILITY (SATURDAY 10:20 P.M.)

Katherine's cell phone ringtone loudly played Abba's "Take a Chance on Me," and Brian reacted, "That's an annoying song."

Scowling at him, she answered the phone, "Hello?" As she listened, a look of fear oozed across her face. Then she screamed, "You asshole! You ruined my life!" Katherine hung up and asked Gus for a shot of tequila.

Karl expressed concern. "Are you okay, Katherine?"

"I'll be fine, Karl. He's such an asshole," she vented.

"Sounds like a real hassle," Brian sincerely interjected.

"Don't worry about it. Men have not been my strong suit, honey. This guy's ruthless. And that song happens to be a classic, you unsophisticated piece of shit."

Brian responded, "At least you have Karl."

"I'm her cousin, numb-nuts, and I'm here to protect her from that evil Russian bastard," Karl retorted.

Brian nodded, feeling joy at Katherine's potential availability, however unlikely that opportunity seemed. Realizing this was not the time to allow machismo to blur his thinking, Brian resorted to a more passive approach with Karl.

Gus chimed in, "Sounds serious, Katherine. I'll call the cops once the roads clear and get you out of here safely."

"It *is* serious, Gus. That asshole forced me to do the single worst thing I've ever done. I really don't want to talk about it."

Everyone sat quietly, staring at the comforting fire, when Katherine's cell phone rang again. She answered reluctantly, but just listened. After what seemed like an eternity, she hung up, bowed her head, and wept.

"What's up, Katherine?" Karl demanded.

"He called me an 'American whore' and said he's coming here when the snow clears to kick my ass."

"Screw that! I'll kick *his* ass," Brian boasted.

"Igor makes you look normal, honey," Katherine told Brian. "He's a maniac."

"His name is Igor? Like Frankenstein's Igor?" Brian cynically asked.

Katherine only smiled, drawing Brian into her heart. She reached over and ran her soft hand across Brian's cheek. "As Karl said, Igor is an evil Russian bastard."

THE EVIL RUSSIAN BASTARD (SATURDAY 10:40 P.M.)

The massive blizzard had Igor temporarily trapped in his apartment across town. He was sipping on vodka, listening to Beethoven's *Fifth Symphony* and fuming at Katherine's responses. He was a simmering kettle ready to boil over.

Igor was a forty-one-year-old Russian immigrant, physically gifted with good looks, grace, and strength. At first glance, this strikingly handsome man, standing at six-foot-two with an alluring smile, attracted women. But he was an out-of-control womanizer and a narcissistic asshole. Igor represented a highly ironic dichotomy: he was a skilled ballroom dancer, and he was a former Chechnyan rebel who violently fought in several conflicts. He was formally trained to gracefully maneuver his body in various forms of dance and in the art of efficient human extermination.

As the clock ticked away into the early morning hours, Igor continued to drink vodka. His determination intensified, and he planned to head to Gus's Place to lethally harm his latest female conquest when the snow let up.

NON GRATUM ANUS RODENTUM
(SATURDAY 11:00 P.M.)

As Igor drank and fumed across town, Brian sat in Gus's Place and took another sip of his Chianti. He glanced to his right, surprised to see an elderly gentleman sitting at the head of the bar, as if he mystically faded into the scene in virtual silence. Brian checked his watch: eleven p.m. sharp. He gazed at the tall but frail-looking white-haired man, wondering why he would be in a place like this on a night like this.

As Brian stared, the old man asked, "What the hell are you looking at, you sorry piece of human defecation?"

Brian smiled. "Excuse me, sir. Could you please watch your language? There's a lady here, and she's very sensitive about vulgarity."

The old man retorted, "Not my problem, dickhead."

Katherine looked at Brian. "I'm confused by your sudden concern for proper language."

With an admiring smile, Brian nodded. "Touché."

With the clandestine arrival of the old man, the proverbial full house was situated at Gus's Place. Gus turned down the jukebox and flipped on the TV to get a weather update. These five diverse individuals would not be leaving this fine establishment on this frigid, snowy evening.

Gus announced, "Okay, I'll keep the bar open as long as you like, and I'll get some hot food up and running for you. I have blankets and pillows in the back whenever you're ready to hit the hay. I've been through this rodeo a few times. We'll be fine."

"I'll take that cheeseburger deluxe deal you've got, Gus, and keep the Chianti coming," Brian blurted.

The others followed with their orders.

Brian removed his heavy white hoodie, revealing a conspicuous and seemingly tasteless tattoo of a rat on his right forearm.

The old man glanced over. "You were a tunnel rat in Nam?"

"Yes, sir, I was, for four long months," Brian responded proudly. "I was also an infantryman."

"*Non gratum anus rodentum*," the old man appreciatively stated.

"That's right, sir."

"What are you two talking about?" Katherine injected curiously. "And how did you know he was in Vietnam?"

"Not worth a rat's arse," the old man responded.

"What the hell are you talking about?" Katherine demanded.

"Hey now, *you* watch *your* language, young lady," Brian said in a parental tone.

"Up yours," Katherine responded, contentious, yet affectionate. Despite the tense start, these two vastly different people slowly began to form a bond.

The old man chimed in. "Not worth a rat's arse. That's what '*Non gratum anus rodentum*' means. It's a Latin term, the motto of the heroic tunnel rats in Nam." He walked over to Brian and gave him a manly hug of appreciation for what Brian experienced. Then he reached out his hand. "Retired Army Sergeant Major Dickie Gates here. It's a pleasure to meet you, my friend. Sorry about the human defecation comment earlier. Sometimes I can be less than charming. I always loved serving next to you jarheads. Let me tell you something. This guy's been through serious stuff."

"Thank you, Sergeant Major," Brian said in a humble tone.

"Please call me Dickie," the old man said, and the machismo-based bond was sealed.

TUNNEL RATS (SATURDAY 11:20 P.M.)

"So, what's the story with these tunnel rats?" Karl asked as Gus interrupted with hot food.

Sensing this was going to be a special night, Gus refilled everyone's drinks. The feeling in the air quickly shifted from contention and hostility to relaxation and unity.

After a robust bite of his Reuben sandwich and a huge sip of beer, Dickie began telling the story of the tunnel rats, but Katherine's ringtone interrupted.

"It's Igor, isn't it?" asked Dickie.

"How did you know?" a surprised Katherine asked.

"I walked in as you were reacting to the previous call. He sounds like a real peach. No respect for people," Dickie told Katherine, assuming the role of elder statesman.

Karl challenged Katherine, "Are you gonna answer it?"

Katherine leaned toward Dickie, then simultaneously placed her elbow on the bar and her hand under her chin. "Nope. Tell me more about those tunnel rats, Dickie."

"Tunnel rats were courageous, but extremely crazy bastards who performed underground search-and-destroy missions." Dickie looked at Brian. "No offense, man."

"None taken, Dickie," Brian responded, feeling reflective.

Difficult memories raced through his mind. Brian vividly recalled the Vietnamese enemies he killed as a tunnel rat, not to mention several others he killed as an infantryman. The bottom line was that killing was killing, even in wartime. No matter how noble and necessary it may have seemed in the context of particular situations, it still involved ending human lives. GI's could place those complex memories in a permeable compartment in the back of their brains, but every now and then, those memories came to the surface. Brian was experiencing as much now, and it showed on his face.

Dickie continued, "Tunnel rats tended to be smaller guys with guts. The tunnels were more than just places to hide; they were virtual underground cities. The tunnel rats' ultimate purpose was to gather intelligence. Additionally, they were sent in to kill any underground enemies and to plant explosives to destroy the tunnels. Tunnel rats were typically equipped only with a handgun, a flashlight, and a knife."

Brian added, "Those tunnels were tight and scary. They had booby traps, and the Cong were sneaky bastards."

"You bet," continued Dickie. "Guys like Brian had to deal with flooded U-bends in the tunnels designed to trap gas. Plus, the Cong guards manned holes on the sides of tunnels and would jab spears through the walls to try to nail our guys."

"And those damned snakes, spiders, scorpions, and bats. I still have nightmares," Brian stated. Everyone listened with interest.

Dickie concluded, "They dealt with some serious adversity. This guy, Brian, is a hero."

Karl looked at Brian respectfully. "Thank you, man."

A tear crawling down his cheek, Brian nodded back appreciatively.

Katherine slid over to the bar stool to her right and hugged Brian to show her admiration. Remaining next to Brian, she kicked off her slippers. She was in a completely foreign place with exciting new feelings. Her soft feel and feminine fragrance blew Brian away.

BRIAN'S AND KATHERINE'S STORIES (SATURDAY 11:45 P.M.)

Shortly after Dickie concluded the compelling story of the tunnel rats, Gus, Karl, and Dickie grabbed blankets and pillows and found spots to sleep as the snowfall continued.

Katherine and Brian stayed at the bar. The fire seemed to get more comforting with each passing moment. Their naturally passionate connection made them feel like they could talk forever. Instinctively, Katherine wrapped her stocking-covered feet around Brian's legs. The simple and affectionate gesture felt so natural and so intoxicating for both of them.

Katherine took another sip of her beer. "What a great night. I like you a lot. You seemed like such an idiot when you first got here, but you're a nice guy. This is one of the best nights of my life."

Brian smiled affectionately, looked deeply into her lovely eyes, and gently placed his hands on her soft cheeks. Admiring Katherine, he wore a sad but satisfied expression.

She was feeling new emotions and wanted this night to last forever. This bizarre little man turned out to be amazing.

Normally, men would make a physical play at this point and try to exploit Katherine for their own pleasure. Brian, though, had no such intention; he told her she was "magnificent." They kissed tenderly for several minutes, floating into their own universe.

Katherine affectionately gazed at Brian. "What's your story, Brian McNerney?"

Brian resisted, but Katherine insisted, and he related a complex tale of challenges. He was born on Christmas Day in 1950 as an only child. His mother died shortly after due to excessive hemorrhaging. That haunted Brian throughout his life, with no help from his father, who had subtle ways of reminding him from time to time.

Katherine asked how he was able to deal with his feelings over the years.

"My life has been a series of uncomfortable destinies. I don't know how else to describe it." His father, the son of Irish immigrants, owned and ran a bar & grill in Hell's Kitchen in New York City. The colorful neighborhood had earned a gritty reputation and figured prominently in the New York City underworld, especially in Irish-American organized crime circles. Basically, it was the home of a lot of poor, working-class Irish-Americans. That bar & grill was a solid business venture with one major problem: Brian's father thoroughly enjoyed the alcohol he served. Whiskey was his preference, leading to an eroded liver and his premature death.

Brian, a street-smart kid, was fifteen when his father died. His father's only sibling, Brian's Uncle John, who lived out on eastern Long Island, took his parentless nephew into his home. A good man of simple means, Uncle John, with his devoted wife, raised and cared for their six children. Normalcy personified. Brian tried to fit in with that family unit, but it never felt right. At seventeen, he joined the Marines, served with honor, and became a decorated veteran who killed several enemies along the way.

"So, you actually have killed people?" she cautiously asked.

"Actually, I've *caused* death. There's a huge difference. In my mind, killing someone means you did it maliciously and illegally. I caused death, and I think about it every day. It was always circumstantial—war or self-defense. Please don't think less of me, Katherine."

That experience of actually ending a human life was predictably profound. Brian once said it caused him to discover that he did, in fact, have a soul.

Upon his discharge at nineteen, Brian returned to Long Island, worked as a carpenter, and got married. Two years after his wedding, a drunk driver killed his wife in a head-on collision, leaving Brian McNerney a widower at twenty-one. His zest for life diminished, and he resorted to heavy drinking and raising hell.

With a reassuring smile, Katherine hugged him and headed to the ladies room. Brian then carefully grabbed her cell phone, jotted Igor's number down on a napkin, and put it in his pocket.

When Katherine returned, Brian asked, "So, what about you? What's your story?"

Katherine had a near perfect upbringing as one of five children born into an Irish-Catholic family on Long Island. She was the baby and grew up without a care in the world.

Her mother and father were loving parents, and they provided a nice life for the entire family. Katherine should have lived a great life, but men became her Achilles' heel.

She did marry twice but got divorced both times. Her first husband had a substance abuse problem. He loved to drink and loved drugs, specifically cocaine. After four painful years, Katherine divorced him. She later married another man who was a steady guy with moderate ambition. Things were fine until he got into a serious car accident, leading to a difficult recovery period in which he was prescribed Vicodin, a highly addictive painkiller. He developed a habit of topping that off with a steady flow of alcohol, leading to yet another fine mess and divorce.

Most recently, she'd hooked up with Igor, the attractive, narcissistic, and fertile Russian psychopath who seemed too good to be true. Igor grew up in Russia in a highly dysfunctional and abusive family situation. He developed strong narcissistic tendencies and compulsively controlled and abused the females in his life. His good looks combined with his short-lived charm captivated Katherine, and they had a passionate relationship for several months until Katherine got pregnant. She very much wanted to have that baby, but Igor wanted no part of fatherhood. He eventually bullied Katherine into having an abortion. She acquiesced but hated herself for it and abruptly broke up with Igor.

Overwhelming empathy for this beautiful woman filled Brian. After sharing their stories, they were both overcome with fatigue, so they rested their heads on the bar. As Katherine dozed off, Brian fixed a temporary bed for her near the fireplace. He guided her there, and she fell into a deep, comfortable sleep. Brian threw a few more logs on the fire, headed back to the bar, and took another sip of Chianti.

CHALLENGING IGOR (SUNDAY 1:00 A.M.)

Brian made a daring decision and sent Igor a fiercely challenging text message: *Igor—I'm Brian, Katherine's new man. Stay away, you Russian bitch.*

In this case, ignorance was bliss. Brian didn't understand the full magnitude of how psychotically dangerous Igor was.

A drunken and angry Igor stared dumbfounded at Brian's provocative text message, then responded, *I'll be there in the morning when the snow clears. I look forward to seeing you. You're a foolish moron.*

Brian would deal with Igor in due time. Before his pending morning adventure, he got some much-needed sleep, and Igor simultaneously succumbed to the effects of the excessive vodka.

ANOTHER UNCOMFORTABLE DESTINY (SUNDAY 5:30 A.M.)

Gus's Place was now quiet with the warm fire crackling in the background. Brian woke up to the sound of his cell phone alerting him to an incoming text message.

I'll be there soon. Meet me outside, you piece of shit. Igor.

Igor began his journey to Gus's Place to accomplish his violent deed. Receiving that message was sobering for Brian, and he felt like he was moving in slow-motion. He reached down to his ankle and placed his hand over the bump in his sock to verify the presence of his well-sharpened switchblade. His knife would be a last resort to disable and assume control over Igor. He looked out the front window as a huge snowplow drove by, attempting to clear the road. Scoping out a possible roadside location for his inevitable conflict with Igor, he noticed a few frozen tire tracks from passing vehicles. Brian gathered his wits, devised a strategy, and forced himself to feel invincible.

CONFLICT RESOLUTION (SUNDAY 6:10 A.M.)

The bright blanket of clean white snow outside softly illuminated the cold, dark dawn. Four of the five patrons were sleeping peacefully when Brian McNerney made his second notable entrance into Gus's Place in the past twelve hours.

As Gus and Katherine stared, stunned, Brian stood in the doorway, shivering uncontrollably. The right side of his white hoodie was completely covered in blood. Outside, the flashing lights of an ambulance and a police car added to the commotion.

Gus grabbed an old blanket from under the bar and covered Brian with it. "What the hell happened, Brian?"

"Igor's dead." After a short pause, Brian muttered, "What a crazy night."

"Oh my God!" Katherine blurted. "Please tell me you didn't kill him."

"No, I didn't kill him," a subdued Brian responded.

"Did you cause his death?" she snapped, recalling their earlier conversation.

Brian flashed a humorless smile. "No, I didn't."

A policeman walked in. "Thanks for the 911 call, Mr. McNerney. It looks like he slipped on the ice and smashed his head. The frozen ground is like steel. He took a very severe blow to the skull, which killed him almost instantly."

Brian asked, "Is there anything else I can do?"

"Nope. You've helped more than your share. That was mighty righteous of you, giving him CPR and trying to stop the bleeding. Well done, sir. You should get some clean, dry clothes on. We got it from here. We'll call you if we need any additional information."

THE WALK HOME (6:30 A.M.)

Gus and his patrons watched in amazement as the ambulance and police car sped away. They all experienced Igor's threatening phone calls but never imagined such an awful thing occurred while they were sleeping. On one hand, it seemed like poetic justice, but on the other hand, it seemed tragic. Any human being with any level of compassion would feel bad—even for a piece of shit like Igor.

Gus directed Brian, "Come with me. Let's get you cleaned up and put some dry clothes on you. I have an old set of overalls and a sweatshirt in the back." When they returned, Gus shouted, "I'm putting on a fresh pot of coffee. Anyone interested?"

Karl and Dickie accepted. Brian said he was wasted and was going to walk home, a few blocks away.

"Would you like to come over for a cup of coffee, Katherine?" he asked, insecure as a high schooler asking a pretty young girl to the prom.

"I'd love that, Brian."

Brian and Katherine said farewell to their bar-mates on that sunny, crisp, and snow-covered morning. As they headed down the street and slowly strolled over the virgin snow, Brian gently grabbed Katherine's hand. "Thanks for joining me."

"My pleasure. Well, that was one bizarre first date."

"That wasn't a date. That, my dear, was destiny." After a thoughtful pause, Brian ventured, "But, if I did ask you, would you actually go on a date with me?"

"Yes, I would."

"Okay, then I'm asking. I want to take you out to a real nice dinner and to watch a movie with me."

"That sounds amazing," Katherine responded enthusiastically.

"It's a date. I recently did a carpentry job at Dante's Corner Cuisine."

Katherine exclaimed, "Dante's Corner Cuisine! I hear it's the nicest place in town."

"Every evening as I finished up my work, I'd watch couples, all dressed up, arriving. I wondered if I'd ever be able to experience the same—wearing nice clothes and escorting a pretty lady to a place like that. I guess I figured I didn't deserve it."

Katherine didn't immediately respond, just clutched Brian's arm tighter, rested her head on his shoulder, and smiled. Her smile was beautiful and authentic, the type she hadn't displayed for years. "You definitely deserve it, and I'd be honored to be your date."

They arrived at Brian's home. "Please come in. I'm going to brew you the best cup of coffee you ever had. I'm also going to toast you a killer bagel."

"You know what, Brian? Just coffee will be fine. I think I'll pass on the bagel."

As they sat and sipped, Katherine carefully asked, "I realize this may be a difficult question for you, Brian, but what actually happened this morning with Igor? Did you… cause his death?"

Brian's expression was stoic. "It was like the cop said. He fell and hit his head. Trust me, okay?" Smile turning nervous, Katherine nodded.

When they finished their coffee, Katherine and Brian made love, then went to breakfast at a local diner. They later experienced an incredible first date. After the movie, they drove to the docks in Brian's truck, where they sat holding hands, listening to Tony Bennett, and quietly enjoying the sparkling evening view of Long Island's Great South Bay. After a rocky start, the Ballad of Katherine and Brian actually proved to be a very comfortable destiny.

THE END

The Goddess of Prospect Park Loves Lilies

UNFORTUNATE NEWS

Deborah Schwartz, Director of the Red Cross Office at Kadena Air Base in Okinawa, had the difficult task of informing US Air Force Major Shannon Smithson of a personal loss. It was April 1986, and Shannon was serving as a medical officer in Okinawa with her civilian husband and their two children.

"Major Smithson, I have sad news. My office received a call from the States. Your brother Thomas, passed away."

Stunned into silence, Shannon bowed her head forward, closed her eyes, and firmly rubbed her forehead with the tips of her fingers.

"Are you okay, Major?"

"Yes, thank you, Deborah. What details do you have?"

Deborah informed Shannon that Thomas died in Beth Israel Hospital in New York City, cause of death pneumonia.

Her twin sister recently told her that Thomas had contracted AIDS, but this was still shocking. Shannon was crushed, but she felt relief knowing her brother would be spared the long-term battle countless gay men with AIDS were experiencing. Shannon and her husband decided it would be best if she went to New York alone while he stayed behind with their two children, so she quickly planned her emergency leave.

NEW YORK

Shannon arrived at JFK International Airport on Thursday afternoon and was greeted by her older brother, Garrett Fitzgerald. Their parents had four children: Garrett, thirty-nine; Shannon and Eileen (the twins), both thirty-six; and Thomas, thirty-four at the time of his death. They also had five grandchildren with another due soon. Mr. Fitzgerald had passed away five years earlier.

The adult twin sisters were only about five feet, one inch in stature, but athletic with fierce demeanors. Shannon had curly brown hair and blue eyes, and Eileen had curly red hair and brown eyes. Mom and Eileen still lived in Lindenhurst; Garrett lived in Boston, Massachusetts; and Thomas had lived in Brooklyn until his recent death.

On the ride home, Shannon asked Garrett, "So, how's Mom doing?"

"Understandably, she's a mess, but she'll be thrilled to see you."

Shannon, physically and emotionally exhausted as she looked out the window taking in her old Long Island stomping ground, responded, "It will be great to see her, but I wish it was under better circumstances."

Garrett nodded in agreement. "How's Japan?"

"It's great. The air base has everything we need, and the Okinawans are extraordinarily friendly people. The food is amazing."

"Sounds incredible."

"How's Robin doing?" Shannon asked.

"She's good. The baby's due any day now. After the two miscarriages, we're praying the third time is a charm. I was conflicted about coming, but Robin convinced me, knowing how tight our family is. She's heartbroken about Thomas."

"She's in good hands up there, right?"

Garrett responded, "Absolutely. Plenty of family around, and her mom's staying with her. By the way, Thomas's wake will be on Friday night, and the funeral Mass and burial will be on Saturday. I plan to drive back up to Boston on Monday."

They arrived at their childhood home, greeted by their mom and Eileen. After Shannon settled in, they enjoyed a nice meal and a few glasses of much-needed wine. They reminisced about Thomas's life, and Eileen left to get back to her family.

As a pleasant distraction, Mom played one quick game of Yahtzee with Garrett and Shannon before hitting the hay. The Fitzgeralds had a long tradition of playing when they were together.

PAYING RESPECT

Thomas's Friday night wake and Saturday funeral were well attended. Thomas was a gay man in the eighties, a challenging time when AIDS was viewed as a dreadful plague. He lived in an apartment in the Prospect Park section of Brooklyn, New York. Though his family was keenly aware of his homosexuality, they never openly discussed it. Thomas was not comfortable coming out to his family until after his father's death. Mr. George Fitzgerald was an old-school World War II vet and hard-working electrician who believed in God, country, and family. Although he loved his children dearly, he was uncomfortable with Thomas's sexuality.

Thomas had one very significant partner, Allen. They'd been together for about three years until Allen died from AIDS over a year ago. After Thomas's funeral, the Fitzgeralds invited family and friends to join them at Thomas's favorite local restaurant, the Clamdiggers Saloon.

Several in attendance shared stories about Thomas, both fun and emotional. Two of Thomas's friends from Brooklyn provided a glimpse into his life there. Thomas made a comfortable living as a data analyst, with a full social life. They also mentioned his caring nature and his great culinary skills.

Regina Williamson, the owner of The Clamdiggers Saloon, had her staff bring out a cake "on the house." With a glass of wine in hand, she told everyone, "I'm on the job, but I wanted to have a drink with you in Thomas's honor. I loved him, and I'm going to miss him dearly. We all know what a great person he was, but he was also a great guitar player, and he had a beautiful singing voice."

Regina told everyone that in the '70s, Thomas periodically performed in the room they were sitting in. During that time, her husband Derek was dying of cancer, and he loved it when Thomas stopped by to visit and play a few songs for him out on the dock. Derek would sit in his wheelchair wrapped in a blanket, close his eyes, and take it all in. On one of his visits, Derek and Regina were sitting out on the dock together relaxing. Derek asked him to play their favorite slow song—"Unchained Melody." Although standing was a physical struggle for her husband, they slow danced as Thomas played, the last time they danced together as her husband passed away a few hours later.

As she finished, an emotional Regina looked up. "Thank you, Thomas." Thomas's mom stood, walked over, and hugged her.

Garrett, as the oldest Fitzgerald sibling, got to his feet and jokingly announced, "Okay everyone, even though she clearly loved our brother, Regina is getting ready to kick us out of here in about thirty minutes. So, thanks to all of you for joining us and for sharing those great stories. Please refill your glasses for a few toasts."

After thanking the staff, Garrett proposed three separate toasts. The first was to Mom, expressing the family's love for her. The second was to Shannon, expressing appreciation for her military service. He also mentioned her heroic efforts in Vietnam in 1975 as part of *Operation Babylift*. The final, emotionally charged toast was to Thomas. Garrett struggled at one point, but after taking a deep breath, he completed a brief but powerful tribute to Thomas with the grace and dignity he deserved.

PERSONAL MATTERS

On Sunday, the immediate family had dinner at Mom's house. In true New York fashion, neighbors brought lots of food to the Fitzgerald home: lasagna, baked ziti, corned beef and cabbage, casseroles, desserts. Keeping with Fitzgerald family tradition, they broke out some wine and played Yahtzee after dinner. After they finished, an exhausted Mom went to bed.

The three surviving Fitzgerald siblings discussed Thomas's personal matters. Shannon, who planned to fly back to Japan the following Friday, volunteered to clear up Thomas's personal affairs in Brooklyn. Garrett offered to drive Shannon on Monday and help before leaving for Boston. Eileen had business to take care of in the morning but agreed to meet them for lunch.

Thomas's two friends from Brooklyn gave them the name and phone number of Shelley Zager, who had Thomas's apartment key. Thomas's apartment complex was primarily occupied by gay men, and Shelley was like a den mother to many, earning her the nickname, "The Goddess of Prospect Park." According to his friends, Shelley was having a difficult time handling Thomas's death.

On Monday morning, Garrett and a jet-lagged Shannon headed into Brooklyn. They went directly to Shelley Zager's apartment. Shelley, a quiet and petite woman in her mid-thirties, lived alone. She had a slightly nervous demeanor but a welcoming smile. After cordial greetings, she closed her eyes and wept quietly. The siblings comforted her; then Shelley explained she and Thomas grew close in the past year and that she really cared about him.

Shannon said, "We're so sorry, Shelley. Thomas was an amazing guy, and we're all going to miss him."

Nodding in appreciation, Shelley regained her composure. They then discussed Thomas's personal matters. Shelley generously offered to get a summary of Thomas's financial commitments with the landlord, along with his bills, and provide one amount to pay. She also provided an option for his clothes and furniture: donating them to the Brooklyn Gay Men's Coalition. They thanked Shelley, then headed to Thomas's apartment.

THE LIST

They carefully inserted the key, slowly opened the door, and eased into Thomas's incredibly neat and impeccably decorated abode with several invaluable items. It had a moderately-sized living room, a small kitchen/dining room, and a spacious bedroom with a full bathroom. Nothing was out of place, except for an empty glass with dried milk film and a plate lightly covered with breadcrumbs in the kitchen sink.

Garrett walked over to check out Thomas's wine collection in a wall-hung oak cabinet, noticing a pile of empty Robitussin bottles in the trash can. Thomas must have struggled with intense lung congestion.

Then Shannon spotted a list on the kitchen table. "Wow, check this out. It's a to-do list with ten items. Thomas had drawn a line through the first two: Number one, do laundry, and number two, call Charles. I think it would be cool if we could get the remaining eight done as we're working on his personal affairs."

Garrett responded, "Yes, absolutely. Well, it's ten-fifteen, and I need to head out after lunch. Are there any easy ones we can knock out? How about 'Pick up photos at Photo Mart?'"

A sudden knock on the door interrupted them. Since she'd taken a few days off from work, Eileen arrived early to assist Shannon. She looked around and noticed three photo albums on a shelf across the room. Without hesitation, each sibling grabbed one, sat, and perused them.

Eileen said, "Wow, look at this family photo from 1958. I remember that day. It was Easter Sunday, and we were wearing our new Easter clothes. Mom and Dad look so happy."

Shannon found another interesting photo. "Here's Thomas and Dad when Thomas was leaving for college."

A teary-eyed Eileen reflected, "I really miss Dad, and now Thomas is gone."

Garrett found one in which Shannon and Eileen were wearing cheerleader outfits and Thomas, who stood between them, was uncomfortably wearing a football uniform. "This was around 1963. Look at your hair. You both look like Little Orphan Annie after a windstorm."

Shannon asked, "Remember when we got into those fights?"

Garrett replied, "Oh yeah. The boys were doing a handoff drill while the girls practiced cheers on the side. Two dickheads slammed the ball into Thomas's stomach, and he started crying. Then you two maniacs attacked."

"Tony DeFilippo and Tommy Weiss," Eileen recalled.

Garrett added, "I think you scarred them for life, getting their asses kicked by girls in front of their team."

Shannon said, "I remember you jumping on Tony's back and choking him until he fell to the ground. I tackled Tommy from behind and pounded his back. The coaches pulled us off and abruptly ended practice. Thomas quit that night."

"I've always admired how protective you were of Thomas." Garrett glanced at his watch. "It's eleven-forty, and I need to leave for Boston soon. Sorry I wasn't able to help, but I'm glad I got to see Thomas's place."

"Let's have lunch," Eileen suggested. "There's a great deli nearby, and concerning the list, big brother, the Fitzgerald sisters will get it done."

Garrett laughed at her well-intentioned sibling jab. During their nice lunch, they continued to reminisce about Thomas. Eileen described his final days in the hospital. He became unconscious and was on a respirator. Eileen's husband drove Mom in each day, and she sat with Thomas for a few hours. Eileen stopped by after work and read poems to him, not knowing if he could hear her.

After lunch, Garrett headed home, and the sisters returned to Thomas's apartment. They searched for important documents and found Thomas's checkbook, bank statements, life insurance policy, and his will. The simple will identified Eileen as the executor, which made things easy. They coordinated several appointments, then shifted their focus back to the list. To help with one of the items, they called Shelley to get Allen's mother's contact information. Eileen then suggested they head into the city tomorrow to take care of a few more.

Shannon responded, "The Photo Mart is just a few doors down, so we can handle it before we leave. It's a bit late to get into anything else. We should open a bottle of wine and sample it in Thomas's honor before we leave."

Snapping to attention, Eileen saluted her sister. "I like the way you think, Major Smithson."

They chose a nice bottle of Chianti, poured two glasses, and toasted their younger brother's great taste in wine. They then sat for a little while enjoying the drinks, noshing on peanuts, and talking.

When they finished, Shannon corked the bottle. "We should do this each afternoon as we're wrapping up."

Eileen agreed. "We need to get rolling. There's a boatload of food at the house, and it will be nice to have dinner with Mom."

Once they left, they handled *Item #3: Pick up photos at Photo Mart.*

On the ride home, Shannon looked at the photos. They were from a trip to Niagara Falls. Thomas was there with another man. The photos were typical vacation shots with incredibly scenic backdrops of the mighty Falls, but one shot stood out. Thomas and his companion were hugging and kissing. Both sisters smiled, and then Eileen started to cry.

"Are you okay, Eileen?"

She nodded. "Yes. These are happy tears. I'm glad he had someone in his life after Allen."

MONDAY NIGHT DINNER WITH MOM

During dinner with Mom, the sisters told her about the day, including Thomas's list. It was emotional for her as she learned more about Thomas's life in Brooklyn.

Mom asked, "How many days do you think it will take to get everything done?"

"We can probably get done by Wednesday evening," Shannon told her. "Worst case, Thursday."

Eileen followed up, "Thomas lived a simple life, and he was so organized. His will was very clear in his desires. And he has several absolutely gorgeous decorative collectors' items. We plan to donate his clothes and furniture to charities, but I feel like each of us should take at least one item as a nice memory of Thomas."

Mom responded, "That's a great idea. How are his finances? Do I need to help pay off any debt?"

Eileen gently squeezed her mother's hand. "That's so nice of you, Mom. They appear to be in decent shape. We'll know more tomorrow. Having said that, he took out a $60,000 life insurance policy and clearly established an even split between you, his siblings, and his nieces and nephews."

Mom wiped a tear from her eye. "My God, I still can't believe he's gone."

Shannon broke out the photos they picked up and passed them around. They loved seeing Thomas in such a happy situation, smiling broadly in each photo. Alternating between crying and smiling, Mom looked through them a few times.

Shannon said, "I wonder who the guy is with Thomas."

Mom confidently responded, "His name is Charles, Thomas's friend. The three of us had lunch together in the city before the holidays. He's a really classy guy, and he knows a lot about art."

Mom then held up the photo of Thomas and Charles hugging. "Oh my, I guess they were more than close friends. That makes me happy, especially after all he went through after Allen passed."

Shannon followed up. "Interesting. 'Call Charles' was one of the completed items on his list."

After looking at those photos, Mom seemed rather upbeat. She poured another glass of wine, lit up a cigarette, and did a drum roll on the table. "Okay, ladies, it's Yahtzee time!"

BIG PROGRESS ON TUESDAY

On Tuesday, the Fitzgerald sisters were in high-energy mode. Shannon and Eileen headed back into Brooklyn and arrived at Thomas's apartment around eight with boxes in hand. Their plan was to walk over to the bank at nine to begin the process to finalize Thomas's finances. After, they'd drive into the city to handle a few things, then get things prepared in the apartment for tomorrow's two pickups.

Thomas's bank was within walking distance, so they had time before their appointment to quickly handle *Item #4: Cancel membership at the Royal K Gym* by phone.

Their meeting at the bank went well as they informed them of Thomas's death and got a clear sense of the process to close out his finances once they got a death certificate. While there, they handled *Item #5: Deposit Tax Return Check*.

They left Brooklyn and drove over to Manhattan via the scenic Brooklyn Bridge. Their first stop was at New York University. Shannon ran in to quickly handle *Item #6: Return Library books to NYU*.

Once Shannon returned to the car, they decided to head to the hospital to pick up Thomas's personal items. On their way, Eileen and Shannon pulled over and grabbed a quick lunch from a street vendor—hot dogs with sauerkraut and a knish with mustard. They devoured their NYC delicacies in their vehicle.

Walking into the hospital from the parking area, they both felt grief-stricken knowing this was where Thomas passed away. They called ahead so everything was ready: keys, a comb, some light change, his wallet with about $230 in cash, and a bag with his clothes. When they returned to their vehicle, they sat in sad silence for a few minutes.

In an attempt to lighten the moment, Shannon said, "Let's roll, sister. Those suits aren't going to pick themselves up."

They made their way back to Brooklyn to handle *Item #7: Pick up suits from Bayside Cleaners*.

After that productive trip, they stopped by to see Shelley about Thomas's rent and utilities. Shelley invited them inside, and they sat with her to finalize things.

While they were getting started, Shannon commented on a painting on the wall. "That's beautiful. What kind of flowers are they?"

Shelley explained, "Lilies. My favorite, so versatile. The white lilies in the painting symbolize purity and virtue. Lilies also come in pink, red, orange, and yellow, each with different meanings, and I love all of them." She bowed her head. "I'm so sorry for my behavior the other day, but I'm having a real hard time with Thomas's death. We've always been close, but on the evening of Allen's funeral, Thomas came to my apartment a bit drunk. We sat and talked, and he wound up spending the night with me in bed."

Shannon gasped, and Eileen exclaimed, "What?!"

"It was strictly platonic. We just held each other as we fell asleep. It was so emotional and so comforting. He was such a beautiful man. That happened a few more times until he met Charles. I personally haven't had a lot of luck with men, but in an unusual way, Thomas was my soulmate."

Smiling, the sisters nodded with empathy. The conversation shifted back to Thomas's personal matters. Shelley had everything taken care of with one total amount, and Eileen expressed her appreciation: "Thank you, Shelley. Your act of kindness helped us take care of *Item #8: Pay Utility Bills.*"

A confused Shelley responded, "I'm sorry, Item #8?"

Eileen told her about Thomas's ten-item list.

Shelley responded, "That's fantastic. It's great you've been able to take care of the list while handling his more complicated personal affairs. So, you have two to go? Is there anything I can do to help?"

"No, but thank you," Shannon said. "It looks like we'll be finished tomorrow afternoon after the clothes and furniture pickup. We'll bring the keys to you then, if that's okay."

"Sounds like a plan."

The sisters exchanged hugs with Shelley, then headed back to Thomas's apartment.

Eileen said, "We got a lot done today. How's your jet lag by the way?"

"It was kicking my ass, but I'm good," Shannon answered. "This is important."

"It's ten after four," Eileen announced. "I say we box his stuff in the morning. Let's have a glass of Chianti, then head home. Mom's making her famous London broil."

They munched on peanuts and savored the wine. Tired but satisfied, they discussed tomorrow's plan—arrive around eight in the morning to box up Thomas's decorative items for Eileen's husband to pick up at ten. The Brooklyn Gay Men's Coalition would arrive between two and three o'clock.

There was a knock on the door. It was Charles, the man with Thomas in the Niagara Falls photos.

"You must be Eileen and Shannon."

A surprised Eileen said, "Yes, I'm impressed."

"I'm sorry for your loss. Thomas and I dated a while back, and I loved him, but he ended our relationship after we returned from Niagara Falls."

Shannon stated, "I'm so sorry to hear that."

Charles joined them for a glass of Chianti. "I discovered later that he tested positive for HIV and didn't want to put me at risk. Pardon my French, but he broke my fucking heart."

He then lifted his glass. "To Thomas, my beautiful friend. I miss you."

Eileen smiled, and Charles responded, "My God, you're both more beautiful than I imagined. You could make a gay man go straight." Laughing, he added, "I heard about Thomas's passing and stopped by to say hello to Shelley. She told me you were here, and I'm glad I got to meet you."

Charles finished his wine, hugged the sisters, and said farewell. Eileen and Shannon also finished their wine and headed back to Lindenhurst for a family dinner.

TUESDAY NIGHT DINNER WITH MOM

Mom outdid herself, as everything was beyond delicious. While clearing the table afterwards, Mom sighed. "This is nice. I wish Shannon's family, and Garrett and Robin were here. Speaking of Robin, I talked with her and Garrett this afternoon. She's uncomfortable but doing well."

For dessert, Mom broke out several delicacies from their favorite local German bakery. Afterwards, she said she wanted to hear more about Shannon's Vietnam experience. "I remember you received a medal, but Garrett mentioned it in his toast to you. I vaguely remember the details, but I'm embarrassed to say I know little about the danger you faced."

Getting emotional, Shannon looked at her beautiful mother, then shared the grueling tale of Operation Babylift. "At the end of the war in April 1975, Saigon was about to fall, and an overwhelming mass exodus began. There were an estimated two thousand displaced orphans who had no one to take care of them and nowhere to go."

Eileen asked, "Were they children of the Vietnamese military and American soldiers?"

"Yes, plus children of Vietnamese civilians who had died in the conflict. To address the crisis, President Ford authorized Operation Babylift, which involved sequentially flying an array of cargo aircraft to transport the orphans to safety and eventually match them with families in America, Australia, France, West Germany, and Canada. Well, I was on the first C-5, the largest of the cargo planes. There were about three hundred people on board and, shortly into the flight, a malfunction forced the pilot to crash land onto a nearby rice paddy. The death toll included seventy-eight children and about fifty adults. About 170 of us survived."

Mom clutched her hand to her heart, "Oh my God, Shannon, that's horrible."

"It was, but Operation Babylift was ultimately successful as we airlifted about three thousand orphans to safety and new lives. I was on four additional flights, and I'm proud I was part of it." Mom and Eileen stared at Shannon with admiration. Shannon then chided, "Okay, are we done with these boring war stories? Let's play some damn Yahtzee!"

The phone rang, and Mom answered. Garrett shared the cheerful announcement: a healthy baby boy, eight pounds and seven ounces. They'd named him Thomas George Fitzgerald.

Mom tearfully hung up. "Such wonderful news."

She then held up her wine glass. "A toast to Master Thomas George Fitzgerald. From Ecclesiastes, 'To everything there is a season, and a time to every purpose under heaven: a time to be born, and a time to die.' I know Dad's smiling down from heaven."

WEDNESDAY WRAP-UP

After fighting jet lag all week, Shannon got her first full night's sleep. When they arrived at Thomas's apartment, they boxed up décor for the morning pickup and piled clothes for the afternoon pickup.

Eileen's husband arrived and immediately started carrying boxes out to his truck. As they were boxing the last few items, Shannon discovered two leather-bound books. "Wow, these seem to be Thomas's diaries, and they're both locked. They feel like sacred items. Do you think we should read them?"

Eileen's husband quickly answered Shannon's question as he walked by. "If it was written, it was meant to be read."

Shannon nervously looked at Eileen. "Why don't we think about it?" Eileen nodded, so Shannon put the diaries in her bag.

With that sizable task completed, it was time to have lunch with Allen's mom. After cordial greetings, they enjoyed a delicious lunch and got to know each other. Shannon and Eileen knew Allen casually but had never met his mom. Toward the end, Allen's mom got emotional when the sisters told her they were "pinch-hitting" for Thomas to handle this key item on his list. Being on Thomas's mind made her feel good. She talked about her son and Thomas as a couple, and how happy she was for them, how supportive and loving Thomas was during Allen's final days.

After tearful farewells, Shannon and Eileen departed. They'd just taken care of the very important *Item #9: Have Lunch with Allen's Mom*. They were on the verge of completing Thomas's list, as they had just one item remaining.

THOMAS'S DIARIES

When they arrived at Thomas's apartment, they sipped on coffee, waiting for the moving crew.

Shannon asked Eileen, "What do you think about these diaries?"

"I think my husband was right. We should read them, then share them with Garrett."

Shannon took both out of her bag, handed one to Eileen and opened the other. One diary covered Thomas's life from the sixth grade into early high school, and the other covered late high school into his college years. Both diaries were captivating.

Shannon and Eileen were taken into a difficult journey of the challenges, heartbreaks, and disappointments their brother faced during his early years. Plenty of fun family stories were featured, but also graphic explanations of internal family squabbles. Descriptions of hurtful social and school situations in which he was ridiculed and bullied, particularly in grade school and early high school, also appeared. He described crushes on male classmates and how he hoped to get their attention. He also shared several graphic stories of his sexual encounters in college, most of which were promiscuous and initiated in public places like gyms and spas.

The moving crew from the Brooklyn Gay Men's Coalition showed up, interrupting their reading. They efficiently removed Thomas's furniture and clothes from his apartment. Shannon and Eileen were blown away by how quickly they got the job done. After thanking them, they sat on the floor of the now-empty apartment and discussed Thomas's diaries.

"That was intense," Shannon started. "We damned sure don't want Mom to read them."

Eileen responded, "I'm emotionally spent, and I agree with you—no way in hell does Mom need to know. What do you think we should do with them?"

Shannon suggested, "Since I'm living overseas, why don't you keep them at your home and later ask Garrett if he's interested in reading them? After that, you could destroy them."

"As they say in your world, Major Smithson, ten-four, over and out."

THE FINAL LIST ITEM

It was almost four o'clock, and everything was done, except for returning Thomas's keys to Shelley and completing the final item on Thomas's list. The sisters decided it was time to enjoy another glass of wine. They held back one bottle of Chianti, a corkscrew, some napkins, the can of peanuts they opened, and a few plastic cups.

As they were getting ready to open the bottle, Shannon suggested, "Let's invite Shelley to join us. That will save us a trip to her apartment, and she can enjoy a glass of Thomas's wine with us."

Eileen smiled. "Perfect!"

Shelley happily joined the sisters, who poured her a glass of wine. They made a fun toast to Thomas and his great vintage collection. The sisters again thanked Shelley, then discussed how smoothly everything went.

After a few moments of reflective silence, Shelley asked one last question. "Oh yeah. Were you able to complete all the items on Thomas's list?"

Eileen walked toward Thomas's bedroom.

Shannon also stood. "We still have one to go, and we're going to handle it right now."

A confused Shelley asked, "What is it?"

Eileen walked back into the living room with a beautiful bouquet and said, "These yellow lilies symbolize gratitude. In honor of Thomas—our brother and your soulmate—they are for you. His final task was 'Buy flowers for Shelley.'"

Overcome with emotion, Shelley closed her eyes and cried as Eileen handed her the lilies.

THE END

No Cure for Hatred

A COMMOTION IN THE BUTCHER SHOP

The electronic sign on the wall of the Bed-Stuy Grocery Store's meat department read:

> TODAY IS SATURDAY, MAY 15, 2022,
>
> And today's African Proverb is:
>
> *"No medicine exists that can cure hatred."*

Bed-Stuy was short for Bedford Stuyvesant, an African-American enclave in Brooklyn, New York. The Bed-Stuy Grocery Store had a particularly popular meat department because of its legendary manager, "Bennie the Butcher." He was an old-school meat carver and a short, heavyset black man with a booming voice. Wearing a faded Knicks baseball cap, a white jacket, and a matching meat-stained apron, he stood confidently behind the counter.

An elderly grandmother, her grandson, and Reggie Watkins. a seventy-one-year-old black gentleman, were in line.

In a roughly congenial manner, Bennie shouted, "Lucky number seven!"

Reggie responded, "That's me, Bennie."

Pop! Pop!

Reggie was interrupted by what sounded like firecrackers firing off and a frantic yell, "Shooter!"

Reggie looked to his right, where a white male wearing military gear frantically exited the end aisle, fumbling an assault rifle. Reggie pushed the grandmother and grandson down and ordered them to get behind the counter. As they scampered to safety, Reggie provided a human shield.

THE AFTERLIFE

After two intense, burning jolts of pain raged through his back and chest, Reggie's world faded to black for a moment. Then his vision oozed back. He was sitting on a relaxing bench in a tranquil field covered with fresh green grass. The sky was pure blue, and the temperature was perfectly comfortable with a garden-fresh fragrance in the air.

Off to his left, animals grazed and drank from a pond with crystal-clear blue water. Countless other people were scattered about, sitting on similar benches. A magnificent archway stood in the distance, consisting of a beautiful, spiraling, silver-gray, cloudy mist. It was massive—about fifteen feet high and twenty-five feet wide.

A soothing voice announced, "John Brennan, God will see you."

An angelic female met one of Reggie's fellow sitters and guided him through the archway. Periodically, people were summoned in various languages. Eventually, it was Reggie's turn.

"Reggie Watkins, God will see you."

A man escorted Reggie through the clouded archway into a quiet area with two cushioned white chairs and a table with a pad and pen resting on it.

"Hello, Mr. Watkins. I'm Rodney, your guardian angel. I imagine you have some questions."

"Damn straight I do!" Realizing the tone, Reggie sheepishly followed up, "I'm sorry."

"No problem. I fully understand your concern. You died at the hands of a hateful individual."

Reggie silently stared at Rodney. Like most people, he periodically thought about the Afterlife, and now he was experiencing it firsthand.

"Let me explain our progression of events here in the Afterlife. You have two steps prior to meeting God. First, we'll provide you with visual access to your earthly sendoff from family and friends."

"Wow, I'm not sure I can handle that."

Rodney reassured Reggie, "Don't worry. You'll be fine. After that, you'll need to thoroughly reflect on your entire life. You'll make notes of anything you deem significant for your conversation with God. Questions?"

Focused, Reggie responded, "You said to write down notes of anything relevant. What do you mean, specifically?"

"Identify five or six prominent events and think about the choices you made. Keep in mind God enjoys a good conversation, within time limitations. When you hear his next Afterlife contact announced, you'll need to wrap it up. Oh, and I must inform you about hyper-celestial-focus. This unique power enables you to intensely relive key life events through focused visualization." Rodney paused for a moment. "It's time for your earthly sendoff."

REGGIE'S EARTHLY SENDOFF

After Rodney vanished, a circular blue vapor floated toward Reggie and stopped in front of his face, providing a direct line of vision into the Howard Wilson Funeral Home in Bedford Stuyvesant. The room was filled with family and friends. The church choir sang a beautiful rendition of "Will the Circle Be Unbroken." Reggie, though, could only focus on his remains, lying ominously in an open casket wearing his best suit.

When they finished, the pastor from Reggie's church welcomed everyone and shared a prayer of mourning. He then talked about Reggie. "Thank you for joining us to pay respects to Reggie Watkins. Reggie was a trusted family man. He had a difficult period in his teens but paid the price for his indiscretions and became a productive citizen. He later served honorably in Vietnam and earned the prestigious Silver Star. Here's an excerpt from his citation: 'By his courage, aggressive fighting spirit, and steadfast devotion to duty in the face of extreme personal danger, Private First Class Reginald R.

Watkins upheld the highest traditions of the Marine Corps and the United States Naval Service. Hometown: Brooklyn, New York.' In addition to his dedication to his family and business, Reggie volunteered countless hours working with troubled youths. He was a positive force in our community. We're going to miss this great man who died saving other people, but that reflects how he lived his life, by putting others first."

Fighting back tears, Reggie's distraught daughter Taniyah followed. "My God, where do I start?" She paused to cry, then regained her composure. "I'm having a hard time with this, so I'll be short. Dad was such a caring husband, always making sure my beautiful mom was taken care of, God rest her soul. He was also a devoted father, relentlessly looking out for me. My dad was big, strong, and intimidating, with his shaved head and the small diamond earring in his left ear. My husband, Tommie, often joked with Dad about their private conversation when Tommie picked me up for our first date. I don't know what my father said, but Tommie was on his best behavior. Dad was also an amazing grandfather who deeply loved our three children and was very involved in their lives. Dad, we love you, and we're going to miss you so."

Reggie's best friend, Mike Williams, helped a tearful Taniyah to her seat, then headed to the podium. "Taniyah, that was beautiful. Pastor, thank you for your kind words and for pointing out Reggie's military service. The pastor mentioned Reggie had a difficult period in his teens and he paid for his indiscretions. Well, I was right there with him during that period. I first met Reggie in the seventh grade when my family moved here from North Carolina. During my first day at a new school, Reggie and I got into a fistfight in gym class. We had a good scuffle, but Reggie got the upper hand, as he was bigger and stronger. Our gym teacher sent us to the principal, who immediately chastised Reggie for not properly welcoming me to my new school. He leaned on him hard and made him apologize to me, which he did. Reggie was an authentically good person and we remained tight from then until that horrible day.

"Reggie would want me to mention Mr. Thomas Cornelius Bacon, God rest his soul. Me and Reggie were good kids, but we hit a rough patch in our teens. We made several bad decisions and ultimately got arrested for robbery and assault. In court, we fortunately faced an empathetic judge, aware of a new government program focused on the economic revitalization of low-income areas. He sentenced us to six months of community service as laborers with that program. That's when we met Mr. Bacon, a highly skilled craftsman. He took a liking to us and hired us as apprentices. Reggie later started his own successful construction business and never forgot Mr. Bacon."

Mike then paused, scanned the audience, and concluded, "Reggie, you had a positive impact on many people. I'm going to miss Friday nights with you, sipping on Chianti and smoking cigars, among many other things. Mostly, I'm going to miss your friendship. I love you, man."

The elderly grandmother who Reggie saved talked next. "Hello and thank you for letting me say a few words. I never met Mr. Watkins before that terrible day, but I remember him standing in front of us in line and thinking that he looked very handsome and very manly. I happened to be looking for a husband and thought that he would make a good one."

Much-needed laughter sparked throughout the audience, bringing a smile to Reggie's face as he observed from the Afterlife.

She continued, "We were so frightened when we heard the shots and that horrifying scream. Mr. Watkins saved our lives. He literally draped his body between us and that terrible man. We felt relieved when we got behind the counter, but we were so sad when we lost him." The grandmother raised her hands high. "Praise God for Reggie Watkins. Rest in peace with the good Lord, kind sir." Bowing her head, she slowly walked to her seat.

Finally, Bedford Stuyvesant's City Councilman addressed the tragedy his community faced, along with some thoughts about Reggie. "On Saturday, May 15, our community lost eight of God's children, Reggie Watkins and seven others."

Reggie had been unaware seven other people died with him that day. The news saddened him.

The councilman continued, "Since the shootings, we learned that the individual who did this had a heart full of hatred, fueled by misguided members of the media, by power-hungry politicians, and by distorted social media influences. Pray for these imprudent individuals with their perverse intentions. Ironically, on that day, Mr. Bennie Davis from the Bed-Stuy Grocery Store had the following message posted on his electronic sign, 'No medicine exists that can cure hatred.' Reggie Watkins was a great man, who amazingly saved two precious lives while sacrificing his own. Rest assured we're going to do all we can to support the loved ones of the victims. Rest in peace, Reggie."

The pastor said a final prayer, and the choir concluded by singing "When We All Get to Heaven."

When Reggie's visual access faded, he buried his face in his hands and wept.

REGGIE WATKINS'S LIFE

A short while later, he fell into a trance. When he woke, he was greeted by Rodney. "How are you, Mr. Watkins?"

"I'm fine. That was difficult at times, but for the most part, it was really nice."

"I'm glad to hear it. Now it's time for you to reflect on your life, sir, and jot down notes of anything relevant to your upcoming conversation with God. Remember the power of the hyper-celestial-focus will be extreme. We will talk again soon, Mr. Watkins."

Rodney again faded away, leaving Reggie alone with his pad and pen to reflect. Reginald Roy Watkins was an African-American baby boomer, born an only child on January 27, 1951 in Brooklyn, New York. His family's income put them in the lower economic class, but they generally lived a secure and stable life. Reggie's childhood, thanks to his parents, was normalcy personified. He attended public school, participated in various youth sports, and his family attended church together. He was a good kid, but he did recall the first time he got in what felt like big trouble with his parents.

At four years old, he carved his initials on the family's wooden-cased TV set just before his mother and father sat down to watch *The Jack Benny Program*. Although that show was geared toward a white audience, Reggie's parents enjoyed watching it because of their admiration for one of the African-American characters on the show named Roy. Roy was a well-educated, articulate man, not the typical black stereotype seen in many films of that time.

In any case, a few minutes into the show, Reggie's mother noticed his carved initials, and it was not pretty. Thanks to his hyper-celestial-focus, Reggie relived the terrible feeling he experienced, fearing facing the wrath of his parents. He jotted down his first comment for his conversation with God.

Reggie's father was a bus driver in New York City, and his mother worked as a part-time seamstress from home. He'd been devastated once his father passed away prematurely from an inoperable brain tumor when Reggie was just fifteen. Watching his mother struggle to provide for him and his grandmother was heartbreaking. Reggie went through a rebellious period and, along with his best friend, Mike Williams, started drinking, smoking weed, and committing petty robberies, which he made note of on his pad.

As Mike Williams mentioned, they were charged with robbery and assault after breaking into a convenience store. The kind judge gave them six months community service working as laborers. For a teenager, it was a grueling experience, but he felt good that he hung in there and eventually helped his mother financially. Smiling in appreciation of Mr. Bacon and the positive impact he had at a critical point, Reggie jotted down another note.

At seventeen, when he enlisted in the Marine Corps in September 1968, he was so nervous. Reggie graduated from boot camp at Parris Island in December 1968. Private First Class Watkins then arrived in South Vietnam in May 1969, stationed at An Hoa Combat Base as a rifleman. While there, he earned a Silver Star for valor. Tragically, he lost his friend, Dan Bullock, killed one month after arriving in Vietnam. A North Vietnamese unit fired a satchel charge into Dan's bunker, killing him and two other Marines. Dan Bullock was the youngest U.S. serviceman killed in the war, at the age of fifteen. He lied about his youth to join the Marine Corps. At that powerful memory, Reggie broke into a heavy sweat and wept as he wrote down another note.

Reggie took a quick mental break to regroup, then continued by recalling how great he felt about starting his own business and earning decent money. Meeting and courting Valerie, the love of his life was another highlight. He'd tried so hard to win her over. His mental journey took him through their wedding, buying their first home, and parenting their beautiful daughter. She'd grown up to be an amazing woman, who blessed him with three grandchildren.

He also recalled an unfortunate period, in which he and Valerie faced some marital struggles. Reggie had violated his wedding vows and betrayed Valerie with a foolish affair. Reliving the guilt, Reggie jotted down another note.

He also recalled the difficult conversation he had with Valerie when he broke off the affair. Eventually, they got back into a positive flow, never letting their daughter know about Reggie's unfortunate transgression. Smiling, he recalled the many good times they had from that point on and how much he valued and appreciated Valerie. He thought he would never recover from her sudden, tragic passing after a heart attack three years ago, but he managed to cope. Completely drained, physically and emotionally, he made another note for God.

Finally, he thought about his current situation and how much he had been enjoying life. He played golf several times a week and met with a few friends each Friday night to sip on Chianti and smoke cigars at a local cigar bar. Additionally, his daughter kept him involved with her family, which was a blessing, although he wished Valerie was at his side. Then, boom, he was inexplicably murdered in a grocery store.

After that intense experience, Reggie again closed his eyes, dropped his head, and wept. He could not handle any more and fell into a deep sleep.

A CONVERSATION WITH GOD

A unique fragrance interrupted Reggie's rest: the scent of a Punch Diablo cigar. Opening his eyes, he saw an elderly, brown-skinned man with a shaved head and an unruly beard. He was wearing a white robe, sipping on red wine, and smoking a cigar.

Looking at Reggie, he asked, "That hyper-celestial-focus deal is severe, isn't it?"

A stunned Reggie said, "I'm sorry, but who are you?"

Standing, the man reached his hand out to Reggie. "Hello, Reggie. I'm God. It's nice to meet you." Reggie got up, returned the handshake, and stared for several minutes. "Please, sit down, Reggie. I'm looking forward to talking with you."

A still stupefied Reggie settled down, gazing at God.

"So, what did you think about that hyper-celestial-focus deal?"

Reggie simply said, "Powerful."

At that point, Rodney arrived with a tray with a fresh bottle of Chianti, two empty glasses, and one cigar. He offered Reggie a glass of the Chianti, which he happily accepted. Rodney poured his wine and then handed him the cigar. "It's a Punch Gran Puro, your favorite, Mr. Watkins."

Reggie nodded his approval as Rodney lit his cigar, then commented, "I'll leave the wine and the empty glass on the table. I'll be nearby if you need anything else."

Reggie stated, "So, you're God. You're nothing like I imagined."

"What do you mean? How did you imagine I'd be, Reggie?"

"Well, I guess like all the pictures I've seen over the years—a white man with long hair and a beard, and I surely didn't envision you drinking wine and smoking a cigar."

"My skin color represents a melding of all the races in the world, and like you, I periodically enjoy a nice glass of Chianti and a quality smoke."

Smiling, Reggie joked, "But a Diablo, that's the last brand of cigar I would expect God to smoke. I mean, *diablo* is the Spanish word for devil. That doesn't make sense, God smoking a Diablo."

"Diablo is merely a name. I personally enjoy the Punch Diablo because of its unique and changing flavor. It starts out medium-strength and medium to full-bodied. Both attributes gradually increase in intensity as you smoke, and by the second half, the cigar progresses to medium to full in strength and full-bodied."

Reggie was impressed. "Wow, you really know your stuff."

With a smirk, God shrugged. "I put my pants on one leg at a time just like you, but at the end of the day, Reggie, I am God. Right?"

Reggie smiled. "I get it. I personally prefer these Punch Gran Puros. I have no detailed explanation of why, but I really enjoy them."

God picked up his glass and offered a toast. "To good cigars and wine, and to a life well lived. Welcome to the Afterlife. Cheers."

They touched glasses, took long sips of their wine, and then savored their cigars. God started the dialogue. "May I see your notes?"

Reggie handed them to God and took another slow sip of his Chianti.

"I see you jotted down six items based on Rodney's instructions. I want you to tell me a little bit about each, but please be efficient. We'll be able to spend some time together, but once they announce my next Afterlife contact, we'll need to wrap it up."

Reggie explained why each situation stood out:

"That seemingly innocent childhood mistake of carving my initials in my family's wooden TV cabinet was the first time I knew I did wrong and felt fear about the repercussions. I realized my parents were intelligent, caring people who loved me unconditionally and taught me accountability. That stuck with me my entire life."

He talked about his rebellious teen years and expressed deep regret about any harm he imposed on others. "It was awful, seeing me as a teenager beating that poor man in the convenience store we robbed. I can't believe I did that. I also vividly remembered the lesson I learned from the judge— that there are good and understanding people in this world who will guide you through adversity. Thank God. I mean thank *you.*"

God smiled. Reggie explained how grateful he was for the overall positive impact Mr. Thomas Cornelius Bacon had on him and how that inspired Reggie to do the same later in life as a community volunteer. He talked to God in length about his experiences in Vietnam. Of all the experiences he recalled, the hyper-celestial-focus was the most intense during this one, as Reggie relived the overwhelming fear he faced in battle and the devastation he felt when his friend, Dan, violently died at such a young age.

Breaking down, Reggie cried again as he told God about the affair and how terrible he felt about betraying the woman he loved. He emphasized how irresponsible, selfish, and disrespectful it was. He thought about it often, always with tremendous guilt and regret. His final note was about how appreciative he was once he ended the affair and repaired his relationship with Valerie. With an improved mood, he walked through the wonderful times he experienced with his family and friends after feeling like he came back from the dead. He had a full appreciation for all the good things. He also mentioned how difficult losing Valerie had been.

As Reggie concluded, God sneezed.

Reggie spontaneously said, "God bless you." As the words came out of his mouth, they both smiled at the irony.

After taking another toke on his cigar and a sip of his wine, God asked, "So, how do you feel about your life? What did you learn from the hyper-celestial-focus experience?"

The remorse he felt about his misdeeds dominated his response. When Reggie finished, God smiled and said, "You're a good person, Reggie. You lived a good life. I'm now going to explain what happens next.

"There are four tiers, and each is categorized by a color: red, yellow, green, and blue—in ascending order. The key determinant is how well each person used their free will and intellect. People in the lower red tier and those in the upper blue tier go directly to their respective destinies the moment their lives end. The red tier can best be explained as what most people would refer to as hell, except there is no fire. They experience what you just did, except they experience it over and over for eternity. The red tier includes mankind's worst: mass murderers, child molesters, corrupt clergy, dirty politicians, et cetera. And they are stuck there all alone."

"Wow, that's incredible. So, they are forced to repeatedly relive their miserable lives for eternity?"

"Yes, that's correct. Conversely, the blue tier can best be explained as what most people refer to as heaven, and it is beyond blissful. People in this tier can choose to relive any aspect of their lives at any time they want. Otherwise, they exist in a state of pure contentment, and they share the experience with loved ones who also earned access to the blue tier. These are people who used their free will and intellect in the most positive way possible.

"The yellow tier is for people who made more than their fair share of mistakes, but they were not grave in nature. They tend to be stubborn about owning those mistakes. They also experience what you just did, except not for eternity, but as many times as needed until they show sincere remorse. People in the green tier also experience what you just did, but only one time because they quickly and firmly show remorse. After they review their lives through hyper-celestial-focus one time, they are accepted into the blue tier. What do you think, Reggie? I'm sure you have questions."

"What about my wife, Valerie? Is she doing okay? Will I get to see her?"

"You'll find out very soon. I promise you. Is there anything else you're wondering about?"

"What about formal religion? What role do our beliefs play in determining tiers? In other words, can a person who did not believe in formal religion get into the blue tier?"

God explained, "Yes, they can. Systems of belief are all manmade, based on interpretations of documents written by people. Some good and bad people regularly attend church, and conversely, some good and bad people have no affiliation with any formal religion. You do not have to attend services to earn entrance into the blue tier. Corrupt ministers who used my name and what I represent for personal gain, however, go directly to the red tier. What else would you like to know?"

Reggie responded, "Why is there so much hatred in the world? Not to be disrespectful, but how have you allowed that to happen? Look at me. I was murdered by a man who never met me and knew nothing about me. From what I understand, he hated me and others in that store strictly because of the color of our skin."

"I probably sound redundant, but by my design, human beings around the world are born with free will and intellect. Those two powerful forces influence how the events of mankind unfold, based on choices people make. As I mentioned, people in various cultures believe in different books written by humans to guide their lives. They derive various meanings from those writings, some noble and some corrupt. And that dilemma is often tied to manmade religions, aligned with those many interpretations. To specifically answer your question about hatred, many people firmly affiliate their beliefs with one ideology, and they view others who do not follow that ideology as evil or wrong in nature. The same goes for people who don't look like them. They often try to harm or even eradicate those others."

"That makes sense. It also seems that extreme thinking, either way, is sort of a cause for evil and hatred."

"Great point, Reggie. Simply put, moderation is the key. Many people fail to peacefully coexist due to extremism."

At that point, the comforting voice from above announced in Spanish, "Miguel Rivera, *Dios te verá ahora.*"

"Well, it looks like our time today is coming to a close," God said. "Are you curious about anything else? Like who shot JFK? Earlier, I had a guy actually ask how Lyle Lovett got to marry Julia Roberts."

"Okay, I'll bite. Did Oswald act alone, and how did Lyle Lovett get to marry Julia Roberts?"

God gave two quick answers, "Oswald did not act alone; he was hired by the mob. And concerning Lyle Lovett, the answer is simple: Women love musicians."

"What about the '69 Mets? How did they manage to win the World Series when no one gave them a chance?"

In a very serious tone, God slowly leaned forward and responded, "That's simple. Gil Hodges sold his soul to the devil. He's now in the red tier." A dumbfounded Reggie stared, prompting God to add, "I'm just messing with you. The Mets won with pitching and defense."

After a good laugh, they quietly finished their wine and cigars. Reggie looked away for a moment, then realized he was alone.

Wondering what was next, he heard a lovely and familiar female voice. "Could you please pour me a glass of wine, Reggie?" His beautiful wife, Valerie, was sitting in the chair across from him, holding the empty glass Rodney left.

Stunned, Reggie immediately stood up, grabbed her hand, and pulled her next to him. They hugged passionately for several minutes, the most exuberant feeling for both of them.

Reggie gazed into Valerie's eyes. "Wow, this is wonderful. How did you get here?"

Valerie stepped back, folded her arms across her chest, then slightly tilted her head.

"Hey, big fella, I was here first. The question is, how did *you* get here? And you still need to pour me a glass of that wine."

Reggie happily obliged. "Where are we?"

Beaming, Valerie held up her glass. "Welcome to the blue tier. We're in heaven—together and forever. Here's a toast to us and our lives well lived. I love you, Reggie Watkins."

"I love you, Valerie Watkins."

THE END

The Magnificent Japanese Zamboni Driver

"THE ICEMAN"

"Ladies and gentlemen, please welcome Sam 'The Iceman,' our magnificent Zamboni driver!"

The booming voice of the Sheboygan Colosseum's PA announcer joyfully introduced Shigemi "Sam" Nakamura, a beloved local legend. As the post-tournament crowd cheered fervently, a fist-pumping Sam gloriously drove his impressive ice resurfacing machine onto the hockey rink. The tradition started in 2011, when Sam began working as a part-time Zamboni driver at the end of youth tournaments at the Sheboygan Colosseum. It continued through that fateful cold Wisconsin night—December 6, 2021. Sam had been heavily involved in Sheboygan's youth ice hockey programs for over fifty years, making a profound impact on thousands of local youths.

Sam, a fun and charismatic American-born man of Japanese descent, was healthy and vibrant at seventy-eight years old. When he drove the Zamboni, Sam always wore a red, white, and blue cowboy hat and flew an American flag on the back. While Sam completed the final resurfacing after each tournament, two songs played loudly throughout the Colosseum: "I Want to Drive the Zamboni" by the Gear Daddies and "God Bless the U.S.A." by Lee Greenwood. The crowd knew the words to both songs and passionately sang along as a smiling Sam majestically drove in smooth oval sweeps around the hockey rink.

On that night, Sam completed the task and drove off the ice to the usual standing ovation from the enthusiastic fans. As he drove off, a jacked-up, heavy-duty black pickup truck with conspicuously gaudy chrome rims pulled into the dimly lit employee parking lot behind the Colosseum.

THE JAPANESE INTERNMENT CAMP

Sam's life, which began in a Japanese internment camp, was a captivating tale of overcoming challenges through perseverance and serving others with love. Sam's father was a highly successful lumber exporter in Japan in the 1930s. His North American connections led to an invitation to work for a large American paper company based in Oregon. In early 1940, Sam's parents and their then three-year-old son, Sam's older brother, moved to Oregon. They lived an affluent lifestyle and appeared to have a bright future in America... Until Dec. 7, 1941, when Japan attacked Pearl Harbor, and the United States finally entered World War II.

In response, President Franklin D. Roosevelt's adminis-tration authorized the evacuation, relocation, and internment of 120,000 Japanese Americans, out of fear that they might support Japan in the war. The Nakamura family's ideal world was shattered. They were forced to move to a life of uncer-tainty at the Heart Mountain Relocation Center in Wyoming, also known as the Heart Mountain World War II Japanese American Confinement Site.

Adjusting to life in the "camp" proved to be difficult. The austere living conditions were far from comfortable. All the detainees lived in a fenced-in area of camp covering 740 acres of dusty land secured with barbed wire and nine guard towers. The 650 buildings and structures included about 450 barracks. At its peak occupancy, over ten thousand detainees filled the camp.

Heart Mountain detainees worked in various capacities to make the community function. Educating the children was challenging, as books, supplies, and classroom furniture were difficult commodities to obtain. Teens and young adults gravitated toward activities like sports and social gatherings.

Initially, local residents questioned why allowing a group of people the government deemed too dangerous to stay on the West Coast to move to their area could be acceptable. Many local businesses displayed "No Japs Allowed" signs, and the Wyoming legislature stopped detainees from voting in Wyoming. In time, however, those sentiments shifted as the interactions with the camp detainees sparked a local economic boom.

SHIGEMI NAKAMURA

Sam was born Shigemi Nakamura on Dec. 10, 1943 in the Heart Mountain Relocation Center. His older brother gave him the nickname Sam after the fabled "Uncle Sam," since he was the first family member born in the United States. Among the many experiences young Sam had at the camp, ice skating stood out. He learned to walk earlier than most children, and his family would frequently take him to the camp's makeshift ice-skating rink.

Early on, Sam would wear smooth-soled shoes and stagger erratically on the ice with the balance of a drunken old man. Eventually, after gaining confidence, he learned how to run and slide with enormous joy. One of the security guards, who loved to watch a smiling Sam playing on the ice, brought him a used pair of children's double-bladed ice skates, and Sam was hooked. He quickly mastered those and moved up to single-bladed skates. Ice skating and ice hockey would become lifelong passions for him.

Sam spent the first twenty-three months of his life at the Heart Mountain location, until it closed in November 1945. After a difficult transition period, Sam's family received a stroke of good fortune. Sam's father reconnected with his former American employer in the lumber industry. He received an offer to relocate to Sheboygan, Wisconsin, working at a box factory.

SHEBOYGAN, WISCONSIN

Sheboygan is located on the western shore of Lake Michigan at the mouth of the Sheboygan River, about fifty miles north of Milwaukee and sixty-four miles south of Green Bay. It is a city with a rich history and is known as the "Bratwurst Capital of the World." Sam's childhood there was fairly routine, although he did experience his share of bullying due to his smaller stature and Japanese origins. That toughened him and motivated him to gain strength any way he could. Sam, who grew to be about five-feet, eight-inches tall, became an avid weightlifter. He also developed street-fighting skills, as he refused to back down to anyone, especially obnoxious classmates who tried to demean and harass him. Simply stated, Sam didn't take crap from anyone.

In addition to his exceptional strength and fitness, Sam grew into a ruggedly handsome young man in his teens. He had a masculine physique, a thick head of straight black hair, and a captivating smile. Sam's passion for ice skating led him to the world of ice hockey, where he excelled in the various local youth programs up through high school. Over the years, he earned a reputation as an excellent skater, who was tough as nails.

Sam's strong physical presence combined with his athletic prowess on the high school ice hockey team led to him meeting the love of his life, Angela Romano. The first time she watched him play hockey, she developed a mad crush on Sam. His good looks, masculinity, and fun demeanor drew Angela to connect with Sam, who fell for her the moment they met. Angela was petite with dark skin, long brown hair, and beautiful green eyes. Their attraction was physically electric, emotionally satisfying, and intellectually stimulating.

Angela was the daughter of Italian immigrants who owned Romano's Italian Restaurant in downtown Sheboygan. To outsiders, Sam and Angela appeared to be an odd match, but they eventually became soulmates. Once their relationship was firmly established, they spent much of their spare time helping Angela's family at the restaurant. Angela's parents adored Sam and introduced him to authentic Italian food. They also later taught him how to savor and appreciate good wine, especially their favorite vintage, Chianti.

Sam graduated from high school in June 1962, then attended college for two years. His plan was to earn his teaching degree, teach high school, and coach ice hockey. He also planned to marry Angela once firmly established in his teaching career. Unfortunately, Sam's father prematurely passed away after a difficult bout with brain cancer. Things got tight financially, so Sam quit college and joined the service.

VIETNAM

Sam enlisted in the Marines in August 1964 and was sent to Vietnam in July 1965 when President Johnson ordered fifty thousand additional ground troops. Sam participated in Operation Starlite, which launched on August 18, 1965 with about 5,500 U.S. Marines attacking the First Viet Cong Regiment. In that violent six-day operation, Sam thrived and earned the prestigious Silver Star.

Like all veterans of combat, the young Sam Nakamura faced death several times and had countless other life-changing experiences—some positive and some negative. Sam was one of approximately thirty-five thousand Asian Americans who served in the Vietnam War. Though he enlisted out of financial necessity and a desire to see the world, patriotism was his primary driver.

As successful as he was in the Marines, he did face his share of discrimination. For example, he often felt excluded from several cliques who did things together like playing cards, drinking, smoking cigars, and performing music. A few times, higher-ranking officers referred to him using derogatory racial slurs. Those challenges were, at times, traumatic for Sam, but he learned from them and moved forward with a positive outlook.

BACK TO SHEBOYGAN

Sam was discharged from the Marines in July 1966, and he used his VA benefits to complete his college education and earn a degree in history in the summer of 1968. Shortly after graduation, he landed a teaching job at Sheboygan High School, initially volunteering as an assistant ice hockey coach at the school. He later married Angela, and they bought a home and had a son, Anthony. Sam began voluntarily supporting local youth hockey programs in the early seventies and continued to do so throughout his life.

Over the years, Sam earned his way to a paid assistant coaching job and, in 1990, became Sheboygan High's head ice hockey coach. He would hold that position until he retired from teaching in 2011. Along the way, Anthony married and had a son named Leo. Sam, a pillar of the community, was loved and respected by many. Among his many contributions to the local community, his involvement in youth ice hockey programs was paramount.

However, on some occasions, he encountered questionable treatment due to his Asian heritage. For example, one evening after working at a youth tournament, Sam and Angela went to a local diner for a piece of pie and a cup of tea. As they sat comfortably in a corner booth having a pleasant conversation, a drunken customer walked past them and chided, "Damn Japs. They need to go back where they came from."

Sam and Angela looked at each other with expressions of mutual understanding, quietly finished their pie, and left with dignity.

RETIRED LIFE

Sam and Angela were both sixty-eight when Sam retired from teaching and coaching. Over the years, their sensible life-style enabled them to live comfortably as retirees. In addition to travel, Sam and Angela had several outside interests keeping them busy and vibrant, although the pandemic years were difficult. Sam absolutely loved his part-time gig as the Zamboni driver for the final ice resurfacing after youth tournaments.

Almost every Tuesday night, Sam and Angela had a beautiful and romantic routine. Angela's parents had passed away several years ago, so the family sold their restaurant, still vibrant under new ownership. Sam and Angela would grab a quiet table in the back corner of Romano's and enjoy an amazing Italian meal with a nice bottle of Chianti.

On one such Tuesday evening in April 2021, their grandson, Leo, and his wife pleasantly surprised them by joining them at their table. Sam waved down a waiter to take their orders. He then poured Leo a glass of Chianti and attempted to pour one for Leo's wife, but she stopped him.

"No, thank you, Ojisan. I can't drink right now."

A surprised Sam responded, "Is everything okay? Are you sick?"

"No, I'm actually quite good. We're going to have a baby."

Immediately, Sam and Angela stood up and hugged both of them. It was a beautiful moment.

Leo explained, "We just found out, and we're so excited. It looks like the due date is December 6, 2021—four days before your birthday, Ojisan. How about that?"

Holding up his glass, Sam proposed a toast. "To our family's beloved next generation!"

AN UNFORTUNATE CONFRONTATION

The months from that toast at Romano's Italian Restaurant to the baby's due date seemed to fly by, and the pregnancy was smooth and uneventful. Along the way, they did a gender reveal and learned they were going to have a son. On the evening of Monday, December 6, 2021, Sam headed out to the Sheboygan Colosseum to watch the final game of a youth tournament, and then handle his post-game ritual—driving the Zamboni. Angela, who frequently went to games with Sam, chose to stay home in case Leo and his wife needed help.

As Sam drove onto the rink, that familiar booming voice announced over the PA system, "Ladies and gentlemen, please welcome Sam 'The Iceman,' our magnificent Zamboni driver!"

Sam superbly completed the evening's final ice resurfacing as the crowd enthusiastically sang along to their two theme songs. Meanwhile, in the parking lot, a black pickup truck pulled in behind the Colosseum. The truck had a gun rack with three high-powered rifles mounted over the rear window, along with two large flags flying off the bed: an American flag and a Confederate flag. Two young white males wearing camouflage hunting gear and masks to conceal their faces were inside.

After finishing his task, Sam exited the Sheboygan Colosseum into the frigid winter evening.

The two young men who had driven up in the truck had been drinking, and they were agitated and angry. Instantly, they confronted Sam.

"What the hell are you doing working here, old man? Can't you see you don't fit in around here?"

Sam calmly replied, "Hey, look, fellas, I'm just getting off from work, and I'm tired. I don't want any trouble."

One of the young men struck Sam behind his legs with a wooden baseball bat. A screaming Sam fell to the frozen ground on his side. The second young man kicked him in the head twice, rendering him unconscious. For good measure, they each kicked Sam's upper torso, then ran away laughing.

The first one abruptly stopped, turned around, and

shouted, "That's what you get for taking our jobs, you Asian immigrant piece of shit. Go back where you came from!"

They jumped into their pickup truck and tore out, wheels screeching. Fortunately, a few minutes later, a maintenance man exited through the same door and discovered Sam. He promptly called 911, and Sam was rushed to the local hospital.

THE NEXT GENERATION

Sam remained in a coma in the intensive care unit for three days with Angela at his side. The local paper reported the attack the next day:

> "One of Sheboygan's finest citizens, Mr. Sam Nakamura, who is 78 years old, experienced a cowardly attack outside of the Sheboygan Colosseum last night. Nakamura coached the Sheboygan High's Ice Hockey Team for 21 years and is now a legendary Zamboni driver at the Sheboygan Colosseum. From what we know, based on security video footage, two masked men driving a large black pickup truck attacked Sam with a baseball bat and then kicked him into submission. Sam is currently in a coma at the Aurora Medical Center. Authorities are aggressively trying to locate the assailants. Please keep Sam and his family in your thoughts and prayers."

One day prior to his seventy-ninth birthday, Sam woke up. He was in bad shape with broken ribs, a concussion, and massive bruises all over his body. He was also experiencing dizziness and blurred vision.

An overwhelmed and distraught Angela sat and talked with Sam. "How are you feeling, Sammy?"

Stunned and tired, Sam asked, "What happened? Who did this to me?"

"You were attacked by two guys outside the Colosseum, and you've been in a coma for the past few days. The police are still investigating. They told me they're confident they can find them. They were caught on video camera yelling racial slurs at you. I guess this 'Asian Hate' business is real."

"Are there any updates on the baby?"

"Not yet, but it should be any time now."

Shortly after, Sam went into a deep sleep. He woke up the next morning greeted by Angela's comforting voice, "Good morning, Sammy. Happy birthday."

"Wow, I'm seventy-nine years old. How about that?"

"How are you feeling?"

"I'm tired and sore, but I'm still kickin'. It beats the alternative."

Breakfast arrived, and they ate together as they watched an alarming local TV news story:

"The Sheboygan Police reported early this morning that the two suspects in the vicious assault on Mr. Sam Nakamura on Monday evening are now in custody. Police received a tip that two young men who fit the descriptions of the suspects were in a bar in Howards Grove. They were drinking heavily and discussing their hatred for Asians and other immigrants in the area. Our team also learned over the past few hours, via their social media interactions, that they are involved in at least two white supremacist groups.

We will keep you updated as this situation develops."

Shortly after, Leo called, informing them the baby would be here soon.

Sam quietly said, "It feels kind of surreal that we're going to be great-grandparents."

Angela smiled. "It sure does. I can't believe it. It's also bizarre that you're both in the same hospital at the same time."

The next day, Leo and his wife had a healthy eight-pound, six-ounce baby boy. Leo arranged a visit to Sam's room the day after the birth, just prior to his family's departure from the hospital. Leo entered Sam's room, pushing a wheelchair safely carrying his wife and newborn son.

"Nonna and Ojisan, I'm happy to introduce you to Sam Shigemi Nakamura."

He handed the infant to Angela, who happily wept as she embraced the beautiful boy. After a few minutes, Sam quietly asked to hold the baby. Angela carefully placed him in Sam's arms. Entranced, he tearfully admired his great-grandson and namesake.

A while later, Leo said, "I'm so glad you got to meet the baby. We need to head out and get home so these two can get some rest. Hang in there, Ojisan, and get well. We love you."

Sam waved goodbye, nodding. "I love you too."

As Angela walked them out, she gave an update on Sam's condition. "The doctors are still concerned, especially about his head trauma. He took a couple of very significant kicks to his head. Thanks for your concern; I'll keep you posted. Please drive home safely and get some rest. I love you."

Shortly after Sam met his great-grandson, he said he was feeling very tired and fell asleep for the last time. His aging body was unable to fight off the significant trauma his hateful assailants inflicted on him. As Angela slept in the other bed in his room, he passed away. The news of Sam's passing traveled quickly, devastating the many people who loved and admired him.

Sam's family opted to have a private wake and funeral service with only family and close friends in attendance. During the beautiful event, the people who loved him paid a heartwarming tribute to this great man, but his unnecessary death at the hands of pure human hatred cast a pall over the day.

The general manager of the Sheboygan Colosseum attended. He spent some time with Angela and asked if he could do anything for her and her family. Angela wished some of the youths who Sam influenced over the years could somehow pay tribute to him. Telling her to stay focused on Sam's funeral, he promised to get back to her with a plan.

CELEBRATION OF A GREAT LIFE

On January 16, 2022, a little over a month after Sam's passing, the Sheboygan Colosseum was filled to capacity with cheering youths and their families, who came to pay tribute to Sam Nakamura. The Colosseum's staff worked with Sam's family and put together a tribute video of Sam's life, including his volunteer work with local youth hockey programs. The video concluded with messages from individuals coached by Sam, one from each of the past five decades:

From the 1970s, John Olson, now fifty-seven, said, "When I was about ten years old, Mr. Sam taught me how to move the puck up the ice while maintaining a clear vision of what was ahead of me. He emphasized that it was no different than life itself. Stay focused on the here and now, but also be aware of what you'll face down the road."

From the 1980s, Robby Anderson, now forty-six, said, "Mr. Sam taught me the art of the slapshot when I was about twelve years old. He was not very tall, but man, was he strong. I remember telling him that I could never hit the puck like he did. He simply told me that, like everything else in life, you can get better at anything you want. But he emphasized that you have to work hard at it and never give up."

From the 1990s, Joannie Nelson, now thirty-seven, said, "I was about eight years old and one of only a few girls playing when Mr. Sam taught me how to skate backwards. I remember feeling really scared, but he assured me that I'd be fine, especially if I learned to use my peripheral vision while on the move. It's no different than going through life, he told me. Just stay aware of your surroundings and watch your back."

From the 2000s, Charlie Hanson, now twenty-seven, said, "I was shorter than most of the other players, so I often felt intimidated on the ice. Mr. Sam, who was also shorter than most players, encouraged me to work hard at getting stronger and to use my greatest skill—my speed. He emphasized it's important in life to know who you are, be yourself, and go with your strengths while working on your weaknesses."

From the 2010s, Charlie Wilson, now nineteen, said, "I started playing in these youth tournaments about ten years ago when my family moved here from Michigan. I didn't know anyone, and being one of the few black kids in the league, I stood out. A few times, kids from other towns would make derogatory comments about my skin color which really hurt me. On one particularly difficult night, an older and bigger kid checked me hard into the boards and called me the 'N word.' After the game, I sat alone crying in the locker room. Mr. Sam came in and sat quietly with me for quite a while. He broke the silence by asking if I was okay. He then told me about his early experiences back in the fifties and sixties being the only minority in the youth leagues. He told his father about how bad he felt when the other kids referred to him using derogatory names. His father told him about baseball great Jackie Robinson, the first black man to play in the major leagues, and the many challenges he faced because of the color of his skin. Mr. Sam told me about how Jackie took the 'high road' and handled those challenges with dignity and let his skills do the talking. He then asked if I really loved skating and playing ice hockey. I told him that I did more than anything. Mr. Sam looked into my eyes and said, 'It's not easy, but take the high road with dignity. Work hard at getting better and let your skills do your talking for you. I got your back if you need me.' Mr. Sam hugged me and walked away. I loved that man, and I already miss him dearly. Thank you, Mr. Sam."

Angela sat in the front row with her family simultaneously smiling and crying tears of joy as they watched the moving tribute to the love of her life.

Once the tribute video concluded, a familiar boom-ing voice announced over the Sheboygan Colosseum's public address system, "Ladies and gentlemen, please welcome Anthony, Leo, and Sam Nakamura—three succeeding generations of Sam 'The Iceman' Nakamura, our magnificent Zamboni driver!"

At that point, to the joy of the Colosseum's packed house, Anthony drove the Zamboni onto the ice with Leo riding shotgun, holding Sam, wrapped in a blanket. Anthony and Leo wore red, white, and blue cowboy hats, as did most of the cheering crowd. Getting to their feet, the enthusiastic Colosseum crowd passionately sang along to "I Want to Drive the Zamboni" and then "God Bless the USA."

As they finished, the PA announcer concluded, "Sam 'The Iceman' Nakamura, you are beloved by your hometown, and you will be missed. Thank you for making such a positive difference in our lives, and God bless you."

THE END

Redemption of a Broken Man

NERVOUS ANTICIPATION – AUGUST 24, 1989

Rory Walsh sat nervously in a rented pickup truck on that dark and haunting three a.m. evening in Virginia Beach. Sighing deeply, he considered the dangerous endeavor he was about to undertake. He was parked across the street from the Pappas Brothers Bar & Grill. Once a month, the owners hosted a high-stakes underground poker game in the basement, which attracted a diverse clientele ranging from lower-income to several well-to-do players. They also offered a variety of enticing side plays, supposedly lucrative to the players, but in fact mostly money-grabbing scams.

After each game, the Pappas brothers, armed with handguns, transported the house-money in a locked metal briefcase to their small office building across the street, where they secured it in a safe. The amount varied anywhere from $100,000 to $300,000, depending on how fortune (or perhaps luck) tilted on any particular evening.

Rory was laser-focused on the rear exit door, through which the Pappas brothers would soon exit to deliver that evening's revenue. Briefly, he glanced across the parking lot at his two accomplices, his younger twin brothers, Aidan and Braden. They were lying on the ground up against the building in the fetal position, disguised as hobos. They each held a bottle of MD 20-20 in one hand and a spray can of military-grade mace in the other. Rory's sweaty hands firmly gripped the steering wheel. Momentarily, he considered calling it off but stayed put as he reminded himself of why he and his two younger brothers were willing to face such intense danger.

As he waited, Rory reflected on his broken life. He was first charged with assault when a drunken asshole groped his widowed mother in the family bar in '68. He got lucky, as the judge offered him the opportunity to join the military in lieu of jail time. The countless life-threatening situations he faced in Vietnam periodically haunted him.

There were three important ladies in his life: his beautiful but mentally impaired younger sister, Erin; her seventeen-year-old daughter, Fiona; and his girlfriend for the past fifteen years, Angie. Guilt struck him for stringing that beautiful young lady along and not yet putting a ring on her finger. Most important now was his recently deceased mother, scammed by the Pappas brothers.

He worried about the fact he was putting his two younger brothers in peril. Over the past few weeks, Rory desperately scrambled to find alternative solutions to solve his grave financial problems, but he always came up empty. He also reminded himself he was an ex-con who'd done time for a second assault and getting busted was not an option. They absolutely had to pull this thing off without a glitch.

Finally, he thought about the most profound life lesson he learned from his Uncle Oscar, his chess mentor: *Always be thinking two or three moves ahead of where you are at any given moment.*

WHO IS RORY WALSH?

Rory Walsh was born on October 25, 1950 into a middle-class family. They resided in Cape Charles, Virginia, located at the southern portion of the Delmarva Peninsula. Both of his parents were Irish immigrants, and they opened up a bar and restaurant called Luck of the Irish Lounge. The oldest of four children, his siblings idolized Rory in spite of the challenges he encountered over the years. His younger sister's mental impairment placed enormous stress on their parents. Their father was a raging alcoholic and ultimately died of cirrhosis on Thanksgiving Day in 1965. Rory was only fifteen, but he immediately assumed the male leadership role in the family.

In their late teens, Rory and his brothers earned a bit of a rough reputation, as they were known to get into altercations, rumored to occasionally be involved in petty crimes.

A neighbor once commented, "The Walsh brothers never met a barroom brawl they didn't like."

They all topped six feet and were physically gifted with strength and good looks to go along with the height. Rory was a great athlete in high school, and swimming was his favorite sport. In fact, he absolutely loved being in and around water.

As an alternative to jail following his first assault charge, he enlisted in the Air Force shortly after graduating high school in 1968. He served as a Combat Controller, a challenging field, and he frequently operated in remote, often hostile areas. Rory would act as a one-man attachment to other special forces teams, trained in a wide range of skills, including firearms, scuba, and parachuting. He served in Vietnam, earned the Air Force Cross for heroism, and was honorably discharged in the summer of 1972. His younger brothers soon followed his lead and served in the same capacity.

Unfortunately, Rory again faced adversity shortly after his discharge. Lenny Watkins, a drug-addicted piece of human defecation from his neighborhood, forced himself on his then-seventeen-year-old sister, leaving her pregnant. Enraged, Rory confronted Lenny, beat him into submission, and broke his jaw. This time, Rory was convicted of assault and sentenced to two years in confinement. Due to his honorable service and heroism in Vietnam, his sentence was reduced to six months followed by two years of probation, but Rory was a felon.

He responsibly did his time and worked hard to recover from that unfortunate incident. One month after his release from prison, his niece was born, and Rory made a commitment to protect and support her like a father. Lenny Watkins died of a heroin overdose shortly after Fiona's birth.

Meanwhile, Rory was having a difficult time finding stable employment in the Cape Charles area. After his probation period, he considered moving, but he stayed put to honor his commitment to take care of his mother, his sister, and her daughter. Plus, he was completely enamored with Angie, then an eighteen-year-old waitress at the family bar, and they began a passionate relationship. The beautiful young woman, six years younger than Rory, could absolutely go toe-to-toe with him in any aspect of life. She came from a broken home and was street smart and tough as nails.

In the mid-eighties, Rory bought a humble beachfront home so that his mom, sister, niece, and girlfriend had a proper place to live. Rory was persistent and worked hard to earn money any way he could. Due to his criminal record, most companies and government institutions ruled him out. He preferred not to work at the family's bar but did so periodically out of necessity. He also tried various other endeavors, such as landscaping, auto repair, and home improvement.

Recently, he found steady, fascinating work in the local fishing industry. Rory was establishing himself as a dependable and competent employee, and his future finally seemed bright, but two severe financial challenges struck.

First, Rory's mom died after a devastating stroke. Shortly after paying their final respects at her burial, they discovered her major gambling problem. She had run up a significant debt. She and Uncle Oscar were involved in the underground gambling world in Virginia Beach and got scammed by the Pappas brothers. Uncle Oscar was a disabled World War II vet in his late sixties, who walked with a severe limp. About a month after Rory's mom's death, two goons demanded Uncle Oscar repay their significant gambling debt within two months.

As if that wasn't enough stress, Fiona talked with him at a Saturday family barbeque about her desire to attend college. She was sad and frustrated because she had the grades to get accepted but didn't think it was financially possible. Although Rory's sister was mentally challenged, Fiona was academically brilliant, had ambitions to become a lawyer, and wanted to attend the prestigious University of Virginia. Hardly a cheap date.

THE PLAN

Later that evening, Rory walked over to the family's Luck of the Irish Lounge, now run by his twin brothers. Rory sat on a stool at the corner of the bar and was greeted by Braden, who happened to be working the bar that night. Without asking, Braden poured Rory a glass of Chianti—his favorite.

He took a long, slow sip. "Braden, you are the man. I really need this tonight."

Braden responded, "Hey, man, do you know what's going on with Uncle Oscar? He was recently in here, and two intense-looking dudes sat at a table with him for a little while. They left in a hurry, and Uncle Oscar has been looking nervous ever since."

Rory was cautious. "Hang tight. We'll talk about it in a bit."

A short while later, Aidan and Uncle Oscar arrived and sat next to Rory. "Pour us two glasses of Chianti, kind sir. We need to have a serious talk about a serious matter."

Braden asked, "What's going on? What do we need to talk about?"

"Uncle Oscar is in a bind and needs our help," said Aidan.

Uncle Oscar informed his three nephews about the Pappas brothers. The Greek immigrants were a dominant force in the Virginia Beach underground gambling world, not to mention master scammers. He and his sister (their mother) got caught up in the Pappas brothers' vile world and were scammed. He used to have a standing seat at those monthly games, and their mom would periodically join him. He went on to explain how much he'd love to get revenge on those "Greek bastards."

Sternly, Braden asked, "So, how much do you owe them?"

A sheepish Uncle Oscar closed his eyes and rubbed his forehead. "$42,000 between me and your mom—but hear me out."

All three brothers sat glaring at their uncle for a few agonizing minutes. Rory broke the silence. "You mentioned that you want to get revenge on these Pappas brothers. What exactly do you have in mind?"

Uncle Oscar told the boys about the Pappas brothers' ritual of moving the house-money after card games, then slowly leaned forward. "They could be an easy mark."

"Are you suggesting we rob them right outside their place?"

"I'm just saying it might be a great opportunity for me to pay back the debt they scammed me and your mother into, and we can get revenge on those pricks. I hear the pot is usually at least six figures."

Crossing his arms, Rory smiled. "Okay, humor me, Uncle Oscar. How might we pull this off without going to jail or getting our brains blown out by pissed off Greek gangsters?"

Uncle Oscar told them the games typically wrapped up around two a.m. After everyone left, the Pappas brothers counted and organized the evening's house-money. He provided specific intel on how they placed the money in a metal briefcase, then transported it to the location across the street. The Pappas brothers were control freaks getting on in years, now in their early sixties. Especially with the element of surprise, they could be physically taken down.

Rory interrupted his uncle. "Why would these guys be so risky with that much money? It doesn't make sense."

"As I said earlier, they're control freaks. Plus, they have a delusional sense of invincibility. They really don't believe anyone would dare mess with them."

Captivated, the Walsh brothers spontaneously brainstormed a hypothetical plan to step in and grab the earnings from an upcoming poker game. The brothers maintained a high level of strength and fitness, and they could use mace to temporarily disable them. They'd need bolt cutters, as one of the Pappas brothers always attached the briefcase to his wrist with handcuffs. At that point, they could grab the briefcase, hogtie the Pappas brothers, and head home.

When Rory asked his brothers what they thought, both seemed interested. Rory told Uncle Oscar he was free tomorrow, and he'd like to take a Sunday drive over the bridge to get a firsthand look at the location. The twins agreed. They were going on a road trip.

PRACTICE RUN

The Chesapeake Bay Bridge-Tunnel is an approximately eighteen-mile long, visually breathtaking sequence of structures. It crosses the mouth of the Chesapeake Bay between the Cape Charles area, where the Walsh family resided, and Virginia Beach, where they hoped to pull off their seemingly far-fetched plan. Three sections of bridge held two one-mile-long tunnels in between, enabling passing ships to cross over. So, you drove onto the first section of bridge for several miles, then dropped down into the first tunnel, then drove back up onto the second section of bridge, then dropped down again into the second tunnel, and then completed the trip on the final section of bridge. For those who suffered from gephyrophobia, fear of bridges, the Chesapeake Bay Bridge-Tunnel was a freaking nightmare.

The next day, the three brothers and their uncle drove over to check out the Pappas Brothers Bar & Grill and get a sense of what they might be up against. They parked inconspicuously across the street. Uncle Oscar pointed out the rear exit door at the bar and the building across the street where they stored the money. He also indicated spots on each of the two front corners the streetlights didn't touch, so they were pitch black at night. The brothers talked about how they could safely position themselves to get the element of surprise. Uncle Oscar suggested they could lie there posing as homeless guys.

Once they felt comfortable with the location, they focused on their exit plan. They figured out the fastest route from the Pappas Brothers Bar & Grill to the bridge, then tried it out.

Once onto the first section of bridge, they drove a short way, and Rory stopped at the first of many pull-off locations used for emergencies.

They all got out of the vehicle and leaned over the railing, awed by the magnificent view and the vast magnitude of the bridge. Rory asked his uncle and his brothers if they thought a person could survive jumping off from this point. The guys went back and forth about the dangers and the possibilities. Rory mentioned the water depth ranged from twenty-five to a hundred feet and that the current could at times be strong.

A seasoned and competent swimmer, he concluded, "I can do it with the right gear."

After the discussion, Uncle Oscar, Aidan, and Braden silently reveled in the beauty of the Chesapeake Bay. Rory, however, thoroughly scanned the area below and imagined what it would take to survive a jump and get to shore.

A police car pulled up, and a cop approached them. "Is everything okay here, gentlemen?"

Rory respectfully replied, "Yes, sir, we just stopped for a few to take in the view."

"I get that, but these pull-off points are for emergency vehicles only. Please move on."

"So sorry about that. Let's head home, guys." Rory found it interesting that the police were so quickly aware of them stopping.

They drove to Rory's place in Cape Charles, barbequed some steaks, and enjoyed a nice meal. After they ate, they hung out, sipping on Chianti and smoking cigars while Rory and Uncle Oscar played their weekly game of chess. Oscar, a masterful player, taught all three boys, but Rory took a keener interest in the game and was competitive in his own right.

After completing the game, they had a follow-up discussion about their plan. Uncle Oscar told them the specifics about the next high-stakes game.

Rory chimed in. "Look guys, I'm fully committed to do this. Those fucking Pappas brothers need a good beating, at the least. My concern is getting you two involved. My life's a mess, and I'm dealing with that, but I don't want you two to cross the law. You both have your lives in order with great families, and you're doing a great job running the bar. This feels too risky for you to get involved."

Braden drained his glass and slammed it down on the table, "Rory, you're my big brother. You know how much I love and admire you, bro, but those motherfuckers messed with Mom and Uncle Oscar, and we need to avenge that shit. I'm in!"

Aidan followed up. "Yeah, Rory. You're my hero, but we're doing this with or without you. And let's not forget about Fiona and the University of Virginia."

Nodding slowly, Rory stared into each of his brothers' eyes. "Okay then, it's settled. Let's do it."

Uncle Oscar took a hit of his cigar. They set the date and time and reviewed their plan in detail. Once the date arrived, the Walsh brothers drove over the bridge in a rented pickup truck. They quietly parked and assumed their positions, waiting for the Pappas brothers to exit the bar.

"GO TIME"

After a nervous waiting period, the Pappas Brothers Bar & Grill's rear exit door slowly opened. A complete sense of calm came over Rory. He glanced at Aidan and Braden, who lay inconspicuously, ready to strike.

Preparing to walk to the building across the street, the Pappas brothers scanned their surroundings. They didn't appear to notice Aidan and Braden. As they crossed, Rory started the truck, flashed his bright lights, and drove directly at them. They both quickly turned and reached for their handguns, but Aidan and Braden sprang up and tackled them, then sprayed the mace into their eyes and held them down.

Rory pulled up and jumped out of the truck holding bolt cutters, two washcloths, and rope. He firmly placed his foot on the face of the Pappas brother with the briefcase and cut the cuffs. Aiden and Braden then stuffed the washcloths into their mouths and hogtied them. Rolling in pain, the temporarily blinded Pappas brothers grunted.

The guys all jumped into the truck and took off. They traveled quickly enough to expeditiously get away, but not so fast as to draw unnecessary attention. After about ten minutes of driving, they made the final right turn putting them on Route 13 North, leading through the toll booth toward the first leg of the bridge.

As they hit the ramp, Aidan shouted, "Oh shit, there's a car coming behind us."

Rory maintained the speed limit, recalling how quickly the cop approached during their trial run. He also kept an eye on the approaching vehicle; they were being chased. He pulled into the same emergency stop from their practice run. Rory tossed the truck key to Aiden, then grabbed a duffle bag with a few of his old government-issue military diving gear items: a flotation vest, swim fins, and a sealed, waterproof backpack.

He hurriedly put on the gear, stuck the briefcase in the backpack, and shouted, "Get home safely. Don't worry. I got a plan."

To the amazement of his brothers, Rory jumped off the bridge. Minutes later, their pursuers, immediately followed by a police car with a screaming siren, reached them. Aiden and Braden stood in awe as the two vehicles raced past. Gazing down into the water, they saw no sign of Rory.

Aiden said, "Hey, man, we have to trust Rory. He told us to get home safely and that he has a plan. Let's get the fuck out of here."

A short distance after the final leg of the bridge, the twins drove past their pursuers who were surrounded by police cars. Their tail had tried to outrun the cops—big mistake for them and a huge break for the Walsh brothers. They headed home without further incident.

FOUR YEARS LATER

Rory, looking sharp in his tuxedo, stood at the front of the St. James Catholic Church overwhelmed by the sight of the beautiful lady walking down the aisle in her amazing wedding gown. Glancing to his left, he smiled at his two best men, Aiden and Braden, and his usher, Uncle Oscar. On his right stood Angie's sister, serving as maid of honor, and two bridesmaids, Erin and Fiona. Rory was finally putting a ring on Angie's finger. They exchanged vows in a beautiful ceremony followed by an amazing reception.

About halfway through the event, Fiona sat next to Rory. "Congratulations, Uncle Rory. I'm so happy for you and Aunt Angie."

"Thank you, Fiona. So, how does it feel to be a college graduate?"

Fiona teared up. "It's amazing. I'm not sure how you and my twin uncles managed it, but I appreciate everything you've done for me."

Smiling, Rory hugged his niece. "Now you need to get your law degree and achieve your dream. Who knows? Maybe I'll need your services one day." At her gasp, he chuckled. "I'm kidding. Just stay focused on your studies, and your uncles will take care of the rest. Okay?"

"You're incredible. I love you, Uncle Rory. I'm so happy Mom and I have you in our lives. Thank you."

Rory gently kissed his niece on her forehead. "I'll always have your back, kiddo. Now get out there on the dance floor and have fun."

Uncle Oscar walked up and proclaimed, "Sorry to interrupt, Fiona, but I want to smoke a cigar with this guy."

Grabbing his glass of Chianti, Rory headed to the deck outside with Uncle Oscar. Aiden and Braden, already seated, sipping on Chianti and smoking cigars, greeted them. Oscar and Rory lit up their cigars, and the four men sat together and relished that very special moment.

Uncle Oscar quietly proposed a toast. "To my amazing nephews, the Walsh brothers. You guys saved my life, salvaged your mother's honor, and set Fiona up for life. I'm still blown away that you pulled off that deal with the Pappas brothers four years ago."

"*We* pulled it off, Uncle Oscar," Rory corrected. "You played a big role. When I swam up onshore scared shitless, you were right there to pick me up and get me safely to that hotel room. I vividly remember how nervous we were that there would be a knock on the door and two henchmen would be there to fuck us up."

Uncle Oscar responded, "Yes, and I remember counting the money. It was over $220,000. Amazing. And thanks to those dumbass Greek bastards trying to outrun the cops that night, their place wound up getting investigated and shut down. They never did figure out that we did the heist."

Rory stated, "Well, my ski mask-wearing twin brothers hit those two old bastards so fast and hard, they had no idea what hit them."

Aiden chimed in, "Yeah, I was worried they'd figure out that we did it. I will never forget that moment when you jumped off the bridge, Rory. I was astounded, but I realized you were thinking a few steps ahead, just like Uncle Oscar taught you. You figured it was inevitable that someone would chase us. You have a pair of brass balls, brother."

"Failure was not an option," Rory quietly stated. "But we swore to take that situation to our graves, right?"

Uncle Oscar and the twins solemnly nodded in agreement. Then Rory proposed a toast.

"We did what we had to do. Cheers!"

Braden added, "Rory, you seem to be doing great working with the Baldwin Fish & Oyster Company. Looks like you found your niche, big brother."

Rory took a long drag of his cigar followed by a slow sip of his Chianti.

At that moment, his bride walked up and scolded the Walsh brothers and Uncle Oscar. "So, you're having a private party, and you didn't invite me." She settled herself sideways on Rory's lap. "Can I take a hit of your cigar, Mr. Walsh?"

"Yes, you can, Mrs. Walsh. My God, you look and smell amazing. What did I do to deserve you?"

On that note, the twins and Uncle Oscar headed inside, and the DJ serendipitously played Santana's slow and sensual "Samba Pa Ti." Rory asked Angie to dance, and they privately enjoyed a passionate slow dance.

As they swayed, Angie asked Rory, "How are you feeling, baby?"

"Well, for the longest time I felt broken, but recently I feel…" Tears welling up, Rory paused as he looked into Angie's beautiful eyes. He took a deep breath as he searched for the right word. "Redeemed. I feel redeemed."

Angie kissed Rory on his cheek, held him tight, and rested her head on his shoulder as they thoroughly enjoyed a dance of absolute joy together.

THE END

The Final Exhibit

DAVE'S WAKE

Wrestling with depression and intrigue, Tommy Butler sat in chilling silence, staring at Dave Rucker's remains. Mesmerized by the highly professional cosmetic job done on Dave's head, he tried to make sense of this unbelievable tragedy. Just a few days ago, Dave placed a gun in his mouth and blew his gray matter through the back of his skull, all over the walls of his archaically decorated living room.

Dave's Uncle Joey was called in to identify the remains. In spite of the violent path Dave took in meeting his maker, Joey said Dave's face vaguely seemed to hold a rather content, almost sneering expression. His current appearance—that of a strait-laced, well-groomed citizen—represented the finest of modern undertaking. Tommy found himself contemplating the extreme measures humans take in preparing their deceased for the final rites of passage, burial, and deterioration.

Tommy Butler's current fate had him playing the role of a respectful mourner in O'Grady's Funeral Home, a family operation and a prime example of a successful and persevering capitalistic institution. Funeral parlors are among the most unique establishments in American society, in a league with brothels, psychiatrists' offices, and public latrines. Each, in its own sensitive way, reeks of privacy, yet provides us with an avenue to reveal things we wouldn't dare expose in a more public setting.

At that moment, in that particular funeral parlor, the exposure came in the form of emotional release, mostly directed at the guest of honor, Dave Rucker.

To say this agonizing ritual had diverse attendees would be a massive understatement. Amongst that well-rounded sampling of humanity, one person distinctly stood out. He was a neatly dressed, well-groomed young man in his mid-teens. He sat a few seats to Tommy's right, staring at Dave's body with fierce intensity. His expression represented simultaneous confusion and determination. Tommy wondered who this kid was and why he sat there all alone. He considered stirring up a conversation but passed because he didn't appear to be in a sociable mood. Plus, Tommy was feeling tense and uneasy sitting just a few yards away from an embalmed corpse.

At that point, Tommy's mind wandered, reflecting on his relationship with Dave Rucker—the now *late* Dave Rucker. They grew up together in suburban Long Island, in the shadow of the world's most complex city, New York. Considering their plethora of similar experiences, including their pre-adulthood "programming" in the form of twelve years of Catholic schooling, they probably should have been more alike. But they were actually vastly different, as evidenced by the different paths they led after high school.

Tommy joined the Air Force and spent most of his service time as a mechanic in Europe, while Dave joined the Marines and wound up in Vietnam as an infantryman, ultimately earning a medal for valor. Upon getting discharged, Tommy moved out west, got married, and lived a fairly stable life as the owner of a small antique shop. Dave's post-war ventures were too long and erratic to mention in one sitting. What a character. They ought to make a movie about this guy. It was really incredible how things change.

As seventeen-year-old high school graduates, they were inseparable partners with big plans. They talked about taking on the world together, but reality took over, and they went their separate ways. Since then, their relationship consisted mainly of an occasional letter or phone call.

Seventeen years had passed since high school, as if their lives were intentionally structured into seventeen-year phases. Phase Two (Dave's last) was over. Tommy really admired Dave. What had driven him to do such a terrible thing?

DRINKS WITH OLD FRIENDS

As that profound thought crossed Tommy's mind, likely mirrored in the minds of many of his co-mourners, a hauntingly familiar face appeared directly in front of his. It was Vernon Rucker, Dave's irritating younger brother. Tommy never did like the guy. He was everything Dave wasn't: conservative, consistent, overbearingly dependable, and annoyingly predictable. Tommy really wasn't in the mood to talk with him, but like many of life's unplanned occurrences, he had to display an appropriate façade.

Tommy greeted Vernon, and they nervously exchanged small talk for a few minutes. Contemplating spending an extended period of time with this guy, Tommy's uneasy feeling grew worse.

Within minutes, however, Tommy was pleasantly surprised by the sight of another old acquaintance, Karl Brooks. He was a classmate of theirs during their school days. Tommy hadn't seen him for at least ten years, but he clearly remembered him as a fun-loving, free spirit. He was tall and lanky with a look of awkward sophistication. Some new additions to his image—gray around the temples, a beard, and round, wire-framed glasses—added to the effect. Karl, Vernon, and Tommy sat on O'Grady's uncomfortable folding chairs and quietly chatted about Dave's disastrous destiny. After a while, they decided to sneak out to a local pub to reminisce.

They selected a quaint Italian restaurant located two doors down from the funeral parlor. The typical New York establishment held all the necessities (booze, tables, chairs, bathroom, pool table). Having selected a table in the rear corner of the bar, they agreed to share a bottle of Chianti. Their initial conversation was geared toward their current situations. Vernon was doing well as a sales manager with an appliance company, and Karl was teaching philosophy at a local junior college. They both seemed content, but Vernon's face showed signs of excessive stress.

Karl mentioned that Dave's suicide really stunned him. On that dreadful night, they had attended a Knicks game together. Karl quipped that the Knicks won, so they probably weren't the cause of Dave's suicide. That angered Vernon, but after a short argument, they mellowed out.

Tommy took advantage of that peaceful moment to mention that he was quite shocked himself. Vernon expressed that although he loved Dave dearly, he learned to expect the unexpected from his brother. Dave never seemed to discover what he really wanted to do or become. Karl intervened by stating that very few people ever really did, and besides, because of that unpredictable nature, Dave earned a legendary reputation back in high school.

THE LEGEND OF DAVE RUCKER

Tommy started with a classic tale occurring in their junior year. He remembered it as if it happened yesterday. They were in Health class, listening to a painfully boring lecture by Mr. Jackson, their football coach. That man was a bulldog: hard-nosed, ugly, and mean, with bad breath.

In the middle of the lecture, Dave raised his hand and mockingly asked Mr. Jackson, "Do you have any idea what the hell you're talking about, sir?"

It was incredible! They all assumed Dave's earthly existence would be terminated, but Mr. Jackson was cool. Without even acknowledging the remark, he calmly finished his lecture. The bell rang, and class adjourned. They cruised up the hallway, laughing in a sort of mock celebration. Dave was king of the hill—at least until football practice that afternoon.

That had to be one of Dave's worst experiences ever. Mr. Jackson ran him through a torturous series of exercises—push-ups, sit-ups, the works—while the rest of the team practiced plays. As always at the end of practice, Mr. Jackson gave them a pep talk. During the talk, he told a now exhausted and pathetic-looking Dave to run one more lap, which he did obediently. After completing that final, painful lap, he staggered toward the team as Mr. Jackson wrapped up his speech. Dave stood right next to Mr. Jackson, bent over, and vomited. Fragments spattered on the coach's hospital white sneakers. Silence overcame the area.

On that distinctive note, Mr. Jackson concluded practice.

That seemed to put an end to the subject. In Saturday's game, Dave went berserk. He tied a school record by scoring four touchdowns, and they won big in what was expected to be a tough contest. Everyone assumed this would unquestionably clear things up between Dave and Mr. Jackson. As a matter of fact, in the locker room after the game, the coach appeared to be on the verge of using that scenario as a motivating lesson. But before he could get to the heart of the lesson, Dave stood up, told the coach to "fuck off," and quit the team. He got suspended from school for a week and was barred from the school's sports program for the remainder of the year.

Dave later told Tommy it was one of the most satisfying things he'd ever done.

To cope with that situation, Dave resorted to excessive partying. During that timeframe, he achieved what the boys viewed as one of the most monumental feats in the history of mankind.

Tony Lovella was unquestionably the most feared student in St. Joseph's High School, by students and teachers alike. The senior played defensive end on the football team. Simply put, Tony was a thug—big, rowdy and an experienced street fighter. One night at a school dance, Dave asked Lovella's girlfriend to slow dance while Lovella was in the bathroom. When Lovella came back and saw them dancing together, he flipped out. He challenged Dave to step outside, and Dave accepted, sporting an arrogant smile. They stormed out behind the school.

Dave's facial expression reeked of ease and confidence. Lovella was much bigger and stronger and appeared to be unbeatable. Tommy remembered thinking that if he was Dave, he probably would have apologized and tried to convince Lovella he was merely keeping his girlfriend warm until he got back from the bathroom.

As young men normally did during this sort of ritual, the two of them squared off and sized each other up. Suddenly and without warning, Dave kicked Lovella firmly in the groin. Lovella's face turned purple, and he bent over in intense pain. Dave quickly followed with another kick, this one square in Lovella's face, breaking his nose. Dave then dove on him like an animal, punching furiously. Four young men had to pull him off of Lovella. The victorious underdog's reputation as a legend was galvanized.

As he reminisced, Tommy had Karl and Vernon's undivided attention. They all knew these were just a few of an unending list of incidents which enhanced the allure of Dave Rucker.

Vernon then took over the conversation, describing some of Dave's exploits since high school. He spoke of Vietnam and

Dave's fascination with that whole scene, especially dealing with the fear. Dave seemed capable of accomplishing anything he put his mind to. He completed a master's degree by combining credits from four schools and started a potentially prominent career in the business world, ultimately quitting because of boredom. Vernon also expressed disappointment in his inability to stabilize Dave.

DRAGON BIRDS

Karl, who lately knew Dave better than anyone, redirected the conversation with some inquisitive observations about Dave's tendencies. Dave appeared to revel in simply getting to a particular point in life because he loved to observe. The achievement was to arrive, not to excel.

"I guess that's why a lot of folks considered Dave to be a quitter, but you had to understand the guy. He viewed life as a museum, and he wanted to see all the exhibits. In fact," Karl said, "I wouldn't be surprised if Dave shot himself simply to experience death, to see what's on the other side—the final exhibit."

He continued by mentioning a highly unusual story Dave read a few years ago entitled *Flight of the Dragon Birds*. Written by an elderly Japanese author, it described the lifestyles of the fictional dragon birds. They were incredibly colorful and majestic, flying in a carefree manner without direction. Their existence was merely a constant quest for pleasure. Once dragon birds were satisfied with their earthly experiences, they would willingly dive into poisonous thornbushes, causing instant death and entrance into a euphoric afterlife. In fact, it was actually honorable for dragon birds to die in that fashion. On the other hand, dragon birds that didn't die by their own choice were viewed as failures.

Karl went on to explain the story had a serious impact on Dave. The story was the first thing that came to his mind when he heard Dave killed himself.

THE BOY AT THE FUNERAL HOME

With that bizarre thought, their conversation reverted back to the funeral parlor and present reality. Tommy recaptured the vision of the young boy he saw earlier. He described the kid to Karl and Vernon and asked if they knew him. Looking perplexed, Karl informed Tommy that he was Dave's son. Tommy was shocked, as he thought he knew all about Dave.

"Yeah, Dave knocked up Buddy McLeod's wife, Linda, while Buddy was over in Nam," Karl explained. "Dave was consoling her in her loneliness. Being a recent Vietnam vet, Dave could supposedly 'relate' to Linda's situation. The whole thing turned out to be a hassle for everyone involved. As you can imagine, Buddy was pissed off when he got back, so he beat the shit out of Linda. He also confronted Dave, who beat the shit out of Buddy. Needless to say, the marital situation wasn't looking very bright for the McLeods. After the divorce,

Linda kept the kid, and Dave sent her money when he could. The kid turned out to be pretty strange."

Tommy inquired, "What do you mean?"

"He's different, almost eccentric. He's real intrigued by power and money, which is kind of strange for a kid his age. As a matter of fact, he's upset because he doesn't get any cash from Dave's life insurance policy due to the suicide. I'm really worried about him."

On that somber note, they took their last sips of Chianti and headed back to O'Grady's. When they got there, the situation was the same as when they left—morbid. The kid hadn't budged; he still sat and stared. Tommy went up to the casket, knelt, and stared at Dave. He tried to give the appearance he was praying, but he was actually thinking about the conversation at the bar.

This was truly an incredible man: intelligent, complex, idealistic and, ultimately, out of touch with reality. Heading back, Tommy reclaimed his original seat near the kid. He would chat with him later if an opportunity should present itself.

Tommy must have been sitting there for about ten minutes when the kid casually walked over to the corpse, leaned over, and spat in Dave's embalmed face. He then pointed at him and shouted, "You worthless bastard!"

A quick scuffle followed. A few of Dave's uncles grabbed the kid and took him outside to calm down. The spectacle shocked those in attendance. Mr. O'Grady immediately responded by cleaning up Dave's remains.

Tommy decided it was time to head back to his hotel room.

THE FUNERAL

The funeral, a tense and quiet affair, took place the following morning. Tommy had a flight out early that afternoon, so he couldn't attend the traditional post-funeral social gathering, which didn't bother him a bit.

During the ride to the airport, he reflected on the experiences of the last few days. Dave Rucker was dead and gone. What did the guy accomplish and what did he leave behind? Were Karl's thoughts accurate? Did Dave kill himself to observe another exhibit? What about that strange Japanese story? Would a grown man emulate a fictional bird?

Whatever the justification for his decision to die, Tommy felt no real sadness for Dave Rucker, only disappointment. Like the honorable dragon birds, he chose to die.

THE END

Printed in the USA
CPSIA information can be obtained
at www.ICGtesting.com
LVHW090337110923
757501LV00003B/471

9 798988 156215